"Like a fine meal, *The Lost Art of Mixing* will leave you warm in your belly, full in your heart, and very, very pleased. You might even find yourself going back for seconds."

—TIFFANY BAKER, *New York Times* bestselling author of *The Little Giant of Aberdeen County*

"[Erica Bauermeister] writes with keen observance and wry wit."

—STEPHANIE KALLOS, author of *Sing Them Home*

Praise for the novels of Erica Bauermeister

JOY FOR BEGINNERS

"Bauermeister's mastery of character development and keen eye for description transform what could have been just another sisterhood book into something deeper."

—*The Seattle Times*

"This book is a joy to read. Bauermeister gives us characters who revel in the best of what life has to offer—loving relationships, fine food, good books, and travel—and she writes with keen observance and wry wit."

—Stephanie Kallos, author of *Sing Them Home*

"Deeply moving and quietly insightful, *Joy for Beginners* will inspire readers to tackle their own challenges—and to celebrate the beauty of deep friendships, good food, well-tended gardens, and other daily pleasures that make life worth living."

—*Shelf Awareness*

"Sensual . . . evocative . . . A book designed to fill you up and make you hungry for life."

—*Publishers Weekly*

"*Joy for Beginners* is ultimately a celebration of life; a literary confirmation of the power of friendship."

—Carol Cassella, author of *Healer*

"This is realistic fiction set in our world—and yet there is something subtly magical (and wholly wonderful) about it. *Joy for Beginners* is a pure delight."

—Bookreporter.com

continued . . .

"Moving, touching, wonderfully written, inspiring to read. *Joy for Beginners* takes us on the emotional journeys of seven women seeking to transform their lives, and proves that sometimes what we really need to inspire us to change is a good, firm shove. Erica Bauermeister's prose is evocative and compelling; this book is definitely worth the leap."

—Garth Stein, *New York Times* bestselling author of *The Art of Racing in the Rain*

"Bauermeister has created a cast of textured and nuanced characters who . . . speak to what makes women interesting and enigmatic. Her prose is velvety smooth, revealing life at once mournful and auspicious. Joyful, indeed. Highly recommended." —*Library Journal* (starred review)

THE SCHOOL OF ESSENTIAL INGREDIENTS

"Fans of Maeve Binchy and Laura Esquivel are going to fall in love with Erica Bauermeister's beautiful story. I know I have. *The School of Essential Ingredients* is exquisitely written and heartbreakingly delicious. It's a luscious slice of life . . . and you will enjoy every bite."

—Sarah Addison Allen, *New York Times* bestselling author of *The Peach Keeper* and *The Girl Who Chased the Moon*

"The perfect recipe for escaping from life's stresses, from savoring the delicious ingredients of Lillian's recipes to the calm and thoughtful rhythm of Erica Bauermeister's luminous prose."

—Kate Jacobs, *New York Times* bestselling author of *The Friday Night Knitting Club*

"Food Network fans will devour this first novel about a whimsical cooking school run by a gentle chef with a fierce passion for food." —*People*

"A lush immersion in the smells, tastes, and comradeship of the culinary world." —*Seattle Post-Intelligencer*

"In this remarkable debut, Bauermeister creates a captivating world where the pleasures and particulars of sophisticated food come to mean much more than simple epicurean indulgence . . . Delivering memorable story lines and characters while seducing the senses, Bauermeister's tale of food and hope is certain to satisfy." —*Publishers Weekly*

"A delicate, meltingly lovely hymn to food and friendship. Lillian's kitchen is a place where the world works the way it should. You'll want to tuck yourself into one warm corner of it and stay all day."

—Marisa de los Santos, author of *Falling Together*

"Bauermeister has a gift for writing about food in sensual, evocative terms, connecting the dish's rich flavors not only to her characters' rich histories but also to the reader's inner palate." —Bookreporter.com

"Reads like a yummy bedtime story, with agreeable characters and dreamy dishes." —*The Oregonian*

"A tale where strangers unite over food, each rediscovering their own essence via cooking's wonders and pleasures . . . Bauermeister manages to keep them fresh and their stories enticing through a series of achingly real vignettes and devastating flashbacks. And her cooking descriptions . . . will compel readers to hit the farmers market and run for the kitchen." —*The Seattle Times*

Also by Erica Bauermeister

FICTION

The School of Essential Ingredients

Joy for Beginners

NONFICTION

500 Great Books by Women: A Reader's Guide
with Jesse Larsen and Holly Smith

Let's Hear It for the Girls:
375 Great Books for Readers 2–14
with Holly Smith

The LOST ART *of* MIXING

Erica Bauermeister

BERKLEY BOOKS
New York

THE BERKLEY PUBLISHING GROUP
Published by the Penguin Group
Penguin Group (USA) LLC
375 Hudson Street, New York, New York 10014

USA • Canada • UK • Ireland • Australia • New Zealand • India • South Africa • China

penguin.com

A Penguin Random House Company

Berkley trade paperback ISBN: 978-0-425-26503-1

The Library of Congress has catalogued the G. P. Putnam's Sons hardcover edition of this book as follows:

Bauermeister, Erica.
The lost art of mixing / Erica Bauermeister
p. cm.
ISBN 978-0-399-16211-4
1. Women cooks—Fiction. 2. Friendship—Fiction. I. Title.
PS3602.A9357L67 2013 2012028010
813'.6—dc13

PUBLISHING HISTORY
G. P. Putnam's Sons hardcover edition / January 2013
Berkley Books trade paperback edition / November 2013

PRINTED IN THE UNITED STATES OF AMERICA

10 9 8 7 6 5 4 3 2 1

Cover photographs: Woman © Helen King / Corbis; Man © Stefano Scata / Getty Images;
Kitchen © Zubin Shroff / Getty Images.
Cover photomontage by Sarah Romeo.
Interior text design by Amanda Dewey.

For Rylan, who sees the stories in things

Every truth has two sides.

—*Aesop*

PROLOGUE

Lillian stood at the restaurant kitchen counter, considering the empty expanse in front of her. It was a Monday morning at the end of December and the restaurant held the calm that occurred only after the onslaught of holiday feasts, the culmination of a culinary season that began in the fall. In those months of ever shorter days, sometimes the only ingredients Lillian's customers could be bothered to take from their own kitchen cabinets were boxes of macaroni and cheese, bread for toast, and the restaurant provided both memory and inspiration—golden half-globes of squash awash in butter, a lamb shank braised with the patience it would take to get through winter. After the exhilaration that was summer in the Pacific Northwest, autumn was like the sigh of an adolescent who realizes he must indeed grow up. It was Lillian's job to remind the people who sat at her tables that being an adult, the passing of a season or a year, was about more than just being older.

Still, Lillian thought, sometimes it was nice to be in the hush of an empty kitchen, without the heat of the ovens, the extra bodies of prep cooks and dishwashers and bussers and servers. This was what fed her—this moment of stillness, the long, cool stretch of the counters and the give of the thick rubber mat beneath her feet.

She decided she'd make a chowder, something simple and nourishing to take for her end-of-the-year appointment with Al, her accountant. Al wasn't quite old enough to be her father, but in many respects he had acted as one for her—a steady hand and mind when she was first opening the restaurant and a dispenser of reliable advice in the eight years since. Their nonfinancial conversations revolved mainly around food; Lillian didn't know too much about Al's wife, and his silence regarding children led her to believe there were none. Al always seemed happiest when he was sitting at a table in the restaurant, or eating the lunches she brought to their appointments in his office. It was a small thing she could give him in return for all his insights, and she was glad to do it.

Lillian collected the salt pork and butter and heavy cream from the walk-in refrigerator, thyme from a pot on the windowsill, dried bay leaves from a glass jar in the row arranged along the wall. She turned on the heat under the pot and added the salt pork, which softened and began to brown. Her stomach grumbled; she remembered she hadn't eaten breakfast and cut a slice of bread, taking occasional bites as she sliced through the hard white flesh of the potatoes.

She removed the cracklings from the pot and added butter and chopped onion, the smells rising up—onion never her favorite thing in the morning, but sometimes a chef didn't have a choice. She poured in chicken stock and then dropped in the potatoes, bringing the liquid to a boil and stepping away while they cooked. No point in pot-watching.

She returned to the walk-in refrigerator, using the intervening minutes to assess the food inside while her mind played with menus for the week. Leftover roasted red peppers and zucchini could be the beginnings of a pasta sauce; extra polenta could be sliced and fried in butter and sage. For all the glamour of restaurants, the underlying secret of the successful ones was their ability to magically repurpose ingredients, a culinary sleight of hand that kept them financially afloat and would have made any depression-era housewife proud.

Sensing the time, Lillian grabbed a package wrapped in butcher paper and headed back out to the prep area. The chunks of potatoes had softened. She smashed one against the side of the pot to thicken the broth, and then unwrapped the package.

As the white paper folded back, the smell of cod rose

sinuously toward her, briny and green, the essence of old fishing nets and ocean waves. Nausea rolled up from Lillian's gut; she took one look at the fish and bolted for the back door.

Outside, she stood at the top of the stairs, gulping in the cold winter air.

"What was that?" she said to herself. And then she stopped and looked down at her stomach.

"Oh," she said. "*Oh.*"

The BOOK *of* RITUALS

When Al was a child, his mother was always showing him books with shapes in red and blue and yellow and green. Triangles. Squares. Circles, she said, pointing. But what he really liked were the shapes his mother called numbers—the way the tall stick of a 1 seemed to be hiding its face from the elegant contours of the 2, the way the grandmotherly 3 nestled up to the stick-and-starch lines of the 4. Al's mother reminded him of a 7. If she had had bigger feet, she could have been a 2, he thought, but his mother always seemed to be floating a bit, or leaning—against a countertop in the kitchen, the wall of the living room. Never quite sitting, never quite straight.

Over the weeks of Al's fourth summer, his mother taught him about counting, using ten straight sticks they collected from the backyard. Al paid attention dutifully, but he still thought that perhaps his mother had it all wrong. The straight sticks had their own purposes, but it was so much more fun to let your eyes slide up and around the slopes of a 9, the banister-curl of a 6. Even if you broke all the straight sticks up into tiny pieces, you could never re-create those curves.

The year Al turned five, his parents divorced and his mother relocated the two of them to Los Angeles. Compared with St. Louis, a land of thunderstorms that cracked the skies wide open and of snow that stopped the world into quiet, Los Angeles was almost overwhelming in its constancy, Monday passing the baton of hazy blue skies to Tuesday with unwavering tenacity. As Al's mother drove him around the city, checking out one apartment after another, Al began to believe that the buildings, the streets, the people, were like the weather, each one indistinguishable from the one before it, everything in shades of gray and beige.

It was like living in fog, Al thought as he stared out the car window. He remembered one night, not long before everything had fallen apart; he had snuck into the living room when his parents thought he was sleeping. They had been watching a movie where there was a lot of screaming and fog and a bad man who would come out of it and hurt people. But the heroine was smart; she found her way home by counting the doors along the street until she came to her own.

So Al began to count.

It was relaxing, he found. 6 buttons on his shirt and they were ready to go. 15 miles on the odometer, one clicking over to the next, and they were at their destination. It didn't matter that the destination looked no different from the other (9) apartments they had seen. The same (14) exterior steps from the first- to the second-floor units, the same (6) kitchen cabinet doors. Al couldn't figure out what his mother was looking for but one day they entered an apartment courtyard and his mother simply stopped.

"This is it," she said. Al looked up at her. There were 3 sparkling stones at the corner of her glasses. A curl had come loose from the waves of her hair and dangled across her forehead.

"OK," he said. He liked that word. It was solid and simple and stood on its own two feet.

LIFE IN ST. LOUIS had been leaf-drenched sycamore trees outside his bedroom window. A yard with grass that only got more and more green during the week, until Al's father went out on Sunday afternoon and the lawn mower roared into life, cutting the grass in long, straight rows, back and forth, back and forth, turning green into a smell that stayed on his father until he showered, an event that was always too far in the future for Al's mother and too soon for Al, who would follow his father around, breathing in the scent of sweat and gasoline and the moment when tall grass became short.

Los Angeles was a tiny apartment with a nook of a kitchen. Al's mother slept on the foldout couch, and often Al did as well, for the bedroom, where she had carefully made the bed with his favorite sheets and painted the walls a friendly blue, still seemed too far away for him most nights. He didn't like the idea that there was nothing between his mother and the front door.

In this new city, Al's school was 3 blocks away. His mother would walk him in the morning, telling him he would have fun that day, although he wasn't sure either of them believed it. He would spend the morning with the other kids, drawing pictures of houses (which he didn't have) and families (ditto). Sometimes they played with puzzles whose pieces were made of numbers, and Al leaned into their familiarity with relief. More than once, his teacher had scolded him when she found the 7 hidden in his pocket. She told him the numbers belonged to all the children, but he didn't quite believe her. He could tell they cared only for the sound of the piece clicking into place. They didn't understand the way numbers could hold your life in their curves.

ONE NIGHT IN JANUARY, as Al's mother was tucking him into bed, she told him she had gotten a job.

"The thing is," she said, "it's a special job and I need to be there in the evenings. But you're a big boy." She brushed his bangs back from his forehead. "You'll be okay by yourself. I'll leave you dinner on a plate and then all you have to do is eat and put yourself to bed and when you wake up in the morning I'll be here."

Al wanted to tell his mother that he wouldn't be okay by himself—that OK stood on its own 2 feet but all he wanted to do was curl up next to her on the couch. After his mother left that first evening, he stood in the middle of their apartment, listening carefully to the noises around him. He counted the cars and trucks driving by on the road until rush hour turned them into a stream too fast and thick for numbers, then he listened to steps walking along the corridor and the click of the lock as old Mrs. Cohen entered her apartment next door. It was quiet in Al's living room, the only sound the ticking of the baseboard heater that his mother said would eat his coat if he left it nearby.

The bad man in the movie always found people by their breathing. They would be hiding, in a shed or behind a door, and the bad man would hear the air racing in and out of their lungs and he would move forward, a smile slowly forming on his face. Al tried to stop breathing, but it didn't work—and no matter all the other sounds of the world outside, you could still hear it.

Al looked around the living room and spotted the

pink vacuum cleaner propped against the closet door. His mother hadn't even unplugged it in her hurry that day. Al knew he wasn't supposed to touch the machine, but he went over and flicked its switch and the roar blocked out everything else. He released the handle the way he'd seen his mother do, and lined the machine up carefully, aiming at the other side of the room. Then he started pushing it in a straight row, back and forth across the green of the carpet.

After a while he heard a pounding on the door. He tried to ignore it, but it didn't stop and he finally turned off the vacuum cleaner.

"That thing's been going for over an hour." Al recognized Mrs. Cohen's voice.

"Is it too much to ask for a little peace?" she continued.

Al stood, uncertain. His mother had said not to answer the door, but she didn't say anything about questions.

"No," he said.

"Al?"

"Yes."

"Al, I'd like to talk with your mother."

This was not a question. Nor was it something that could happen.

"Al? Are you there?"

"Yes."

"Is your mother there?"

. . .

WHEN AL'S MOTHER had come home that night to find her son sleeping on Mrs. Cohen's big blue couch, there had been a discussion between the two women that Al was luckily too sound asleep to follow. But afterward Al started going to Mrs. Cohen's apartment in the evenings while his mother was at work.

Al loved being at Mrs. Cohen's. Her whole apartment was blue—carpet, furniture, walls, each of them a slight variation in hue until Al felt as if he was underwater or in the sky, or both. She had a long hallway lined with family photographs, and every night she took Al on her "memory walk" as she called it, strolling down the length of the hall while she told him stories about each person. Al liked the small stories best, the ones about her children and husband—the time Rachel put a frog in her mouth, the summer Eli decided he was Captain Hook and walked around for two weeks with his sleeve pulled down over his hand. How Mr. and Mrs. Cohen first met on a ship coming from Europe when he was fourteen and she was twelve; the way he had taught her to sway with the boat so she wouldn't get seasick. Mrs. Cohen would always shift her feet back and forth when she told that story, and Al would join her, feeling the boat beneath them.

Mrs. Cohen cooked, too—beef stew that had simmered all day, pancakes that weren't pancakes but a combination of potatoes and onions and warmth that floated through the apartment and snuck into the pockets of his coat. And something she called a kugel, its name as playful as the smell of vanilla and sugar and cinnamon that came from the oven. But Al's favorite thing about being with Mrs. Cohen was Friday night. When he arrived, the apartment would be filled with the fragrance of chicken soup and there was always fresh-baked bread, its surface brown and glistening, lying in a fancy braid across the counter. At dinnertime, she would light one candle and let Al light the other, and before they ate she sang an almost-song in a secret language just for them. Al didn't know what the words meant, but he loved how peaceful they felt, as if the phrases themselves were setting down the weight of the days behind them. Al looked forward to Friday all week long.

And then, one day when Al was ten, his mother told him they would be moving. He would have a new father, she said. They would live in a house again, wouldn't that be lovely? And it wasn't so far away. But the neighborhood they moved to was different than anything he had seen before—cul-de-sacs lined with white and beige rectangles set low to the ground. No stairs to count, the windows uninterrupted sheets of glass. And worst of all, no Mrs. Cohen, because no matter how many times his mother said they weren't moving far, it was apparently too far to visit, and Fridays were date night for his mother and her new husband. Al would sit in his room with the door closed, trying to talk in Mrs. Cohen's secret language, while the babysitter cooked frozen TV dinners until the apple cobbler transformed into a fruit brick.

Al's math classes were the one place where the world made sense during the eight years that followed. Solve for *x*, the teacher would say, and Al could almost hear the numbers whispering in anticipation, ready to dive under the bar of a fraction, disappear down the trapdoor of a subtraction sign. It could make you feel almost sorry for the *x*, Al thought, with everybody staring at it, concentrating, their only goal to leave it standing alone.

WHEN AL WENT TO COLLEGE, he took classes in accounting. He could have studied mathematical theory; he had been tempted more than once by the silence of a 0, or the challenge of how to hold an imaginary number in your hand. But in the end, the hidden stories in accounting numbers always intrigued him more.

He tried to explain it to the girl he saw reading an Agatha Christie novel over lunch in the cafeteria. She held a tuna sandwich in her upraised left hand, one bite missing from the end. Al liked that about her, the way she didn't just start in the middle.

"Accounting can be like solving a murder, without the

blood," he said. "Give me the numbers and I can tell you why a business died or a marriage fell apart."

She looked at him, unconvinced.

"Can you make money at it?" she asked, her smooth blond hair falling around her shoulders.

"Yes," said Al.

"All the time?"

"You know what they say," he answered, "about death and taxes."

"How do you feel about children?" she asked.

While most of the girls Al had met in college wanted a man who wanted children, it was clear that Louise was not a member of that club. Her question was a gauntlet thrown down on the cafeteria table between them, the price of admission into her life. But Louise alone would be more family than he had come to believe he would ever have.

"I don't need them," he said, although he knew even as he said it that he was wrong.

"I'm Louise," she said, holding out her hand.

YEARS LATER, he would wonder why he had wanted her so badly. Perhaps it was the hair, so blond that the sun would set it glittering. Perhaps it was as simple as the bite out of her tuna fish sandwich, although Al was later to learn that people could begin at the beginning of something for many reasons, and not all of them had to do with respect or kindness. Sometimes they were just being thorough.

By their twenty-ninth year of marriage, Al had come to accept that Louise took the balancing of accounts to a level far more literal than he had ever believed possible. Every gesture and moment of affection was scrutinized, tallied up on the lopsided balance sheet of their union. For weeks at a time he would watch her complaints silently building, making her every word and action brittle, her skin shrinking back from his touch as if refusing to give him something he had not paid for. He waited, feeling the dry heat accumulate in their bed as every night she would turn resolutely away from him. This, her back seemed to say, is not for you.

And then finally, one night, when the unbalance of the accounts finally reached a tipping point, she would turn toward him in bed and the reproaches would begin, one after another, knocking against him, endless as waves on the side of a docked boat. All the small moments of disaffection, the slights and missed opportunities that he hadn't seen. Which he would have seen if he loved her, she knew. The time he could have given her a hand as she was getting out of the car. The way he didn't come over to the stove to help her as she was cooking. The money he could have made if only he marketed himself.

Al would listen, silently. There was no particular point in responding, the cycle so well established that he could only wait for its conclusion, which would come when finally, emptied and slightly euphoric, she would lean over and kiss him and he would accept the sex he no longer felt like having.

A TIME CAME, a Monday morning in March. Al was fifty-one, which perhaps played a role in his increased contemplation of his life and that of others. He sat at his desk, surrounded by towering stacks of papers, personal lives waiting to be formulated into tax returns. Perusing his clients' financial information was like reading a book in a language few people knew. By the time Al had filled in the blanks of the first page of a 1040 tax form, he already knew the security guard who was taking side jobs for cash, the frustration of the woman whose full-time occupation would always be declared a "hobby," the midlife crises of sports cars and boats. Even in the clients who never came to his office, who never sat across the desk with pain splashed on their faces, he saw death in a sudden surge of medical expenses, a lowering in the number of dependents.

People gave him numbers, black marks on white paper, without ever realizing the secrets they were revealing. Al knew without looking what his own numbers would say: one spouse, no dependents. No hidden mysteries, no clues to unravel—the simple form, if ever there was one.

. . .

"I NEED YOU TO pick up a book for me," Louise told him the following Saturday, leaning across the kitchen table to hand him a piece of paper. "I called ahead; they'll have it at the front desk for you."

Al looked down at the note in his hand, the title of the book written in his wife's clear, emphatic handwriting, along with directions to the big bookstore where he had, a few months earlier, bought her Christmas present.

Park on the east side of the lot, she had written at the end of the instructions, *in the shade under the trees.*

As if rereading the note herself, Al's wife nodded suddenly and then reached behind her for the paper towels and pulled several off the roll.

"Sometimes there are birds in the trees," she said, handing the towels to him. "Once it dries on the car it's hard to get off. Make sure you wipe before you drive."

Al stood and pushed the wad of paper towels into his jacket pocket, then got his keys from the hook labeled "Al," by the front door, and went to his car. He had inherited it when his grandfather died, an old 1958 steel-blue Cadillac with fins that seemed to float up into the air. Driving it, he wondered sometimes if it might lift off the ground as he crossed a particularly high bridge. It would take a while before it hit the water below; perhaps it would be streamlined enough to level out, coast on the currents of air, settle into the water and simply continue on. The paper towels would likely get wet, though, he thought as he turned on the ignition.

THE PARKING LOT was remarkably busy, even for a Saturday. But the weather was sunny, unusual for March, and Al didn't mind when the only spot he could find was on the other side of the lot; he walked across the black pavement, feeling the first intimations of heat rise up toward him as he watched a young couple, their hands flying in conversation as if waiting for permission to land on the sweet glide slope of the other's body.

The book was not at the front desk after all. As Al stood at the customer service desk waiting for a young woman to track it down, a portly man with curling white hair and a black fedora walked up and introduced himself to the clerk behind the counter—the bookstore was bustling about them and Al didn't catch the name. The clerk checked the computer screen in front of him and nodded.

"Sure," he said to the man. "We have three in stock. I'll go get them."

And while Al stood, waiting for his wife's copy of *Quick Knits for a Saturday Night* to appear, the clerk sped off and returned with a small stack of books.

"Can I get you a pen?" he asked as he set them down in front of the man next to Al.

The man shook his head. He pulled a shiny black pen

from his jacket pocket, then took the top book from the stack and opened its cover, uncapped the pen, and signed a name in a long, lazy scrawl across the title page. He paused a moment, allowing the ink to dry, then closed the cover and placed the book carefully to one side before repeating the process two more times.

It was like watching a priest bless the head of a small child, Al thought—although the author standing next to him was perhaps more pompous than ministerial. Still, there was a reverential quality to the gesture, as if the book somehow changed its chemical composition through the process, becoming heavier with its newly granted importance. It wasn't until he was back in his car that Al realized the clerk had never asked the author for any identification. The author could have been anyone, really.

"Huh . . ." Al said to himself as he started the car. He drove home, thinking.

THE FIRST TIME, he was terrified at the prospect of getting caught. He chose a relatively unknown author from Idaho, not local but close enough that a drive-by visit would not attract extra attention. He practiced a signature; he even tried smoking in order to lend that authorial smell to his personality, but the only effect was that Louise looked at him sharply and studiously increased the distance between them. In the end, all his preparations were unnecessary. At a bookstore on the far side of town, he introduced "himself." The clerk was mildly interested, retrieved the small stack of two books, and handed them over.

Al briskly picked up his pen and, with a bit of a flourish, scrawled the author's name across the title page, just as he had practiced. He looked up; the clerk was gazing off above Al's shoulder.

Al took the second book, this time more slowly, the surface of the cover hard and shiny beneath his fingertips. He opened it, feeling the binding creak slightly under his fingers, and the world narrowed to the creamy-white expanse of the title page, complete but still waiting—for him, he thought, although he knew that wasn't the case. Still. He lifted his pen and felt his hand move across the slightly rough paper, as if, perhaps, he was writing, as if, perhaps, he was anyone other than himself.

"There we are, then," he said, sliding the books across the counter to the clerk.

"Sure," she replied.

He had done it, he realized. He was going to get away with this.

"Well, you know, I was in town," he said casually. He left the store, forcing his facial muscles into any expression but a grin.

AFTER THAT, it became a game. Every few weeks, Al would select a different bookstore. The small stores were the hardest, the inventory handpicked, the clerks lingering in the aisles like bespectacled drug pushers. He learned quickly which books would be easiest—if a store stocked two or three copies of a title, he was in luck, the author well liked enough that the store wouldn't worry about not selling the books but not so well known as to excite much interest in his appearance.

Meanwhile, at his office, Al watched his clients, noting their expressions. Mr. Walters was particularly educational. Al knew from the numbers that Mr. Walters was most likely contemplating leaving his wife—Al had seen a rise in travel expenses, as well as a significant drop in dividends without a correlating claim of capital gains from a sale, suggesting a new and sunny offshore account for a hefty portion of Mr. Walters's stock portfolio. And yet, Mr. Walters sat next to his wife in Al's office, his face a mixture of mild interest and perfectly ordinary confidence. Al would go home at night and practice the expression in front of the mirror, holding out his hand, speaking his name of the week.

Choosing the book developed its own protocol. He would look over covers and titles, finding one that intrigued him, and then open to the back jacket flap, anticipation mounting, hoping that he might pass for the author in the photo in case anybody checked. If the book felt right in his hands, he would purchase it and carry it about for the next few weeks. When he was ready, he would make his appearance—always at a different store—and then he would start the process over again.

Over the months, as he found that his identity was never challenged, his choice of authors began to slip into new and tantalizing territories. How young or old could he be? What nationality might be too foreign for his face? Once, he even signed a murder mystery by a woman author who wrote under a male pseudonym.

He couldn't have said why he was doing what he was doing, whether it was a feeling of being someone else or more himself—Al with a secret. He knew Louise would never understand, even though she carefully applied makeup and styled her hair each time before she left their home, an act of assumed identity that made no more sense to him than his forgery would to her. But Al knew, too, which of their behavior would be seen as less rational in the court of social opinion—a fact Louise would be sure to point out. And so, he said nothing.

ONE DAY, Al realized he had only one bookstore left in the city—the one where he had first seen the fedora author signing his work. Maybe it was the feeling of a task too soon finished, a bet never called in. Maybe it was the rare sunshine on a late-autumn day, making him feel as if any risk came with an automatic safety net. In any case, Al walked through the big brass-handled doors and up to the customer service desk, surveying the face of the preternaturally young clerk behind it.

"Hello," he said casually, "I'm Mark Twain; I'm here to sign stock if you have it."

The clerk's face lit up in recognition.

"Oh my God," she said, her voice rising. "I've heard of you. Let me get your books."

As Al waited, triumph humming its way through his bloodstream, he wandered over to a group of leather chairs nearby and looked nonchalantly at the books spread across a coffee table. Behind him, he sensed movement, a surge in energy. He glanced over his shoulder and saw the young clerk coming back, accompanied by a manager with an outraged expression.

Al turned back to the coffee table, looking for a hiding place. He grabbed the biggest book he could find and dove deep into a vacant chair, placing the book firmly in front of his face. Behind him he could hear the clerk's voice, bewilderment, the manager's continuing harangue. Apparently, however, Mr. Twain had disappeared.

Al continued to sit, his face set between the pages of the book, his heart slamming in his chest. He hoped the clerk would not be fired; he hoped, almost equally, that he would not be caught. He tried to imagine the consequences; he doubted author impersonation would hold much cachet in prison. But in the end, he thought, whom had he really hurt? The authors had sold more books.

The clerks he encountered had experienced a (more or less) unusual moment in their day. What could be wrong with that? All the same, he resolved to sit quietly until the young woman was gone for lunch. It was doubtful anyone else would notice him. It was an upside of being physically unremarkable for which he was suddenly grateful.

After a few minutes, he sensed the activity in the bookstore returning to normal, and his breathing slowed. His eyes wandered over the words in front of him; a passage caught and held him, something about the nature of time. Al snuck a peak at the title: *The Book of Rituals and Traditions.*

Two hours later, Mark Twain forgotten, Al left the store, the book creating a rather awkward beer belly under his coat.

RITUALS, Al decided, were a lot like numbers; they offered a comforting solidity in the otherwise chaotic floodtide of life. But it was more than that. A ritual was a way to hold time—not freezing it, rather the opposite, warming it through the touch of your imagination. Six p.m. might always be an hour on the clock, fixed and named, but Friday dinner with Mrs. Cohen—the lighting of the candles, her face relaxing over the course of the meal as the sun set outside—that had been something altogether different.

Any moment could become a ritual, Al thought as he

brushed his teeth—in its simplest iteration, a ritual was just a matter of paying attention to a moment in time, giving it a name, a reason. Traditions like Christmas or Thanksgiving gained strength as they were passed down through generations, meanings growing with memories. Rituals, however, could happen every day or be needed only once, never to be repeated—a confluence of human need and creativity, a container for a feeling that could otherwise slip away or eat you alive.

At night in bed, with Louise turned away from him, Al would think about the rituals in the book. They kept him company in their own way, could turn the slope of Louise's body back into a shape and not an accusation. The perfect combination of ritual and person had the beauty of an equation, he realized, the answer changing with the variables, no two alike. It was math, only more so.

At the office, Al found himself looking at his clients, wondering about what ritual might shift the balance of their accounts. He felt full to bursting with the secret knowledge of their lives. He wanted to lift life out of the numbers, reach across his desk toward the people on the other side, help them find rituals that would acknowledge their successes and head off the impending disasters, but he couldn't quite figure out what to say.

IT WAS ALMOST ONE O'CLOCK, and as Al waited for his next appointment, his stomach growled slightly.

Al had met his client Lillian one afternoon some eight years before, just as she was getting ready to open her restaurant. He had been walking to the bank to make a deposit. It was October, raining, and the umbrella over his head made him feel invisible to a world he glimpsed only in quick, private bursts. He had passed the Craftsman house that stood between the movie theater and the bank like some kind of unkempt cousin at a family gathering. It had been remodeled into a bar once, years before, the dream of a software entrepreneur who could have used Al's financial advice, for the business had opened and closed within the space of a year, and for almost a decade the place had been empty, the roof collecting moss while the cherry trees in the front yard bolted and twisted into an unruly sculpture.

But there had been activity over the past few months; the front yard had been pruned and planted, the shingles stained a quiet brown and the porch boards painted a warm and elegant red. As Al walked by that October day, a scent of something he could almost remember floated out toward the street and caught under the dome of his umbrella. Cinnamon? Vanilla? Without thinking, he put his hand on the top of the wrought-iron gate and pushed it open, his feet finding their way down a stone path to the open side door of the kitchen.

The woman inside was young and slim, with dark hair pulled into a quick ponytail. She was alone in the kitchen, which was clean and bright and professional, in contrast to the cozy exterior of the building. She stood at the big stainless-steel sink, wielding a spray nozzle at a mixing bowl. The kitchen was warm from the heat of an industrial-sized oven, the fragrances stronger now, coloring the air.

"Hello?" Al said tentatively.

The woman turned around.

"The smell . . ." Al continued.

"Ah," she said, smiling. "Cookies. I'm celebrating. This is my restaurant. Well, it will be when we finally open next week. I'm Lillian."

She walked across the kitchen, wiping her wet hands on her white apron.

"I'm Al," he said, shaking her hand. "I have an office up the street."

"You're the accountant," she said. She saw the question on his face. "I'll be needing one. A friend told me I could trust you."

She paused, smelling the air.

"Cookies are done," she said. "Would you like one?"

LILLIAN'S RESTAURANT had become a success, helped along in part by Al's financial guidance, and over the years Lillian had become a friend as well as a client. It was Al who, seeing the success of her dinner creations, had suggested that Lillian start teaching cooking classes, and encouraged her to open for lunch, the latter a suggestion he unrepentantly acknowledged as selfish. Al had started eating at Lillian's several times a week at noon, discreetly tossing out the nondescript slices of ham on buttered white bread that Louise gave him to take to work, and ordering a marinated eggplant sandwich with a generous slathering of aioli sauce, or a blackened-salmon salad, the surface of the fish crunching, spicy and hot, between his teeth.

When it was time to go over the restaurant accounts at Al's office, Lillian generally selected a time slot just before or after lunch on Mondays, when the restaurant was closed, and Al knew by now to anticipate food along with Lillian's accounts. She called them his Blue Plate Specials, and Al had decided there was nothing better than the combination of spices and textures and numbers, even if it occasionally left grease on the pages. It took him back to when the smells of Mrs. Cohen's cooking used to linger on his math homework and evenings meant family, even if it wasn't his own. And just as he had never told his mother about what Mrs. Cohen's dinners meant to him as a child, he never told Louise about his new lunchtime routines.

Not that there was anything, in the traditional sense, for Louise to be jealous of—Lillian had always treated Al as a delightful surrogate uncle, a vision Al had accepted with a certain, if not unmixed, relief. Al told himself that he was protecting Louise's feelings—she was so proud of her own cooking—but the reality was, he knew that whatever these lunches added to his side of the equation could only be subtracted from hers.

And yet he needed them—the food, the conversation, the feeling of communion they brought into his day. They were like perfume slipped behind the ear of a beautiful woman, or wine with dinner—nothing you had to have to live, and yet nothing felt more like life than the experience of them.

So when a child-woman dressed in a big gray sweatshirt and worn jeans came dashing into his office ten minutes late for Lillian's appointment, a large manila envelope in her otherwise empty hands, he could only be disappointed.

"I'm Chloe," she said. "Lillian's sous-chef. She asked me to bring these—she's sick today."

She saw his downcast expression. "Oh, damn it," she said. "I forgot the food in my car. I'll be right back."

There was the sound of tennis shoes pounding down the stairs that led to the street, a door slamming. And then a tide pool of fragrance coming up the stairs—butter and bay leaves, thyme and cod and onions.

"Here we go." Chloe entered the office, breathing hard, a bag in her arms. "Don't worry; it's good. I just finished off what Lillian started."

She looked around the office expectantly. "Where should I put it?"

"On the desk, please. Thank you."

Chloe unpacked a round metal container and poured

the soup into a large white bowl, which she set on Al's desk next to a white linen napkin and a big, round spoon. She stepped back and observed the place setting, considering.

"Oh, hell," she said. "The bread." And she was gone again.

Al waited a moment, and then picked up the spoon and carefully tasted the soup. It smelled good, but he wanted his first reaction to be unobserved.

The taste flowed across his tongue, a mix of sea and sky, warm cream and softened onions. Al found himself remembering an afternoon, not long after he and his mother had moved to Los Angeles. They had been on their way to look at an apartment when his mother suddenly turned the car away from the freeway on-ramp and took them instead to the beach. They had sat on the sand, looking out over an enormous expanse of water, unlike anything Al had ever seen. He tried to count the waves but finally had to give up. He asked his mother if they ever stopped, maybe at night, and she said no, and he thought—that's what infinity sounds like.

"Do you like it?" Chloe asked anxiously as she entered, bread in hand.

"Yes," he said. "Very much. Here, sit down. You should have some."

They ate in silence. After a while she looked up from the bowl and glanced around Al's desk.

"What's this?" she said, reaching over and picking up

the big book of rituals that was resting on top of a short stack of file folders. "Doesn't look like a tax book."

"Just something I've been reading," he said quickly. He took it from her and started to walk over to the bookshelf.

"Wait," Chloe said.

Al looked at her for a moment. She sat in the chair, swallowed up by her sweatshirt. She reminded him of a 4, Al thought. Not the kind where all the lines meet up with each other, clean and straight, but the kind where there was a break at the top, a space where life poured in, for better or worse. What ritual might help her navigate the floodtides of her life?

"Why do you have that book?" she asked.

And Al sat down, and leaned across the desk, the book open in his hands.

The

RED SUITCASE

Chloe stood at her front door, looking out at the dark. It was New Year's Eve, almost eleven, and the neighborhood was far from silent. She could hear a party down the block to the right, probably the Morgans, famous in the neighborhood for their raucous, extended-family celebrations. Chloe could hear their voices now when she listened, make out the sound of children staying up long past their bedtimes, the prolonged hiss and sharp pop of the illegal fireworks the relatives bought at the Suquamish reservation on the way into town.

Her own New Year's Eve had been quiet thus far, just she and Isabelle sitting in front of the fire, which Isabelle's age-spotted hands tended with an assurance Chloe could not yet master, mostly because Isabelle refused to give up the task, sitting by the fireplace as if reading the smoke that rose up into the chimney. Almost a year now Chloe had been living in this house—housemate, not guest, she would remind Isabelle. Housemate, not protector, Isabelle would say, looking pointedly at Chloe. True, and not true, on both counts.

Chloe had first met Isabelle in Lillian's cooking class. At that point, Chloe was a nineteen-year-old busser at Lillian's restaurant, the cooking class a first, instinctive step toward a dream of becoming a chef. It was Isabelle who had taken Chloe in when she had left her boyfriend and the thought of returning to her parents' house had quite literally given her hives. Chloe had arrived on Isabelle's doorstep at ten at night, and the older woman had given her homemade chamomile tea, insistent that it would cure the red blotches covering Chloe's arms. Two hours later, the litany of Jake's transgressions diffused into the air, Chloe had looked down at spotless skin. Isabelle set Chloe up in the guest room where she had stayed until they both realized that the arrangement was better than temporary, better, in many ways, than family.

Isabelle loved the dark, Chloe thought as she looked out the front door. When Chloe had first moved in, she would come home from Lillian's restaurant late at night and check on Isabelle, only to discover the house empty. She would finally find Isabelle in the backyard in her yellow men's pajamas and a kitchen apron, gardening by the light of a headlamp, a fairy circle of spades and cutting shears and weeding forks surrounding her. Isabelle said gardening at night was more fun, and better for the plants. You could feel them, she would say: you could tell with your fingers which ones should go, which ones needed to stay. Besides, it made for a better surprise in the morning. Chloe had to admit she was often astonished, looking out the kitchen window as she held her morning cup of coffee, to see a patch of daisies meticulously free of weeds, a row of beans gracefully winding their way up long, white strings.

But recently, Chloe had sometimes found Isabelle gardening out in the dark with no headlamp, no apron, and the surprises in the morning were more often exactly that. Last week, Chloe had come home from work and heard rustling in the yard next door. There had been raccoons recently, and Chloe looked over the three-foot-high fence to check, and spotted Isabelle digging with her spade in the middle of the neighbors' hydrangeas.

It was funny, and not in a humorous way, Chloe thought now, how the qualities you admired most in someone could become your biggest obstacle when things started going off-kilter. When Chloe had first met Isabelle, it was her independence that drew Chloe to her—the way Isabelle kept moving forward even when her memory sometimes slipped her sideways. But nowadays, Isabelle's independence was transmuting into waywardness and Chloe sometimes wondered how long it would be before family would have to be family again.

Still, even on her good days—and probably especially on her bad—Isabelle wouldn't have thought twice about walking out the door at night with a suitcase in her hand. Wouldn't have worried about what might be in the dark, wouldn't have cared what the Morgans might think, or been embarrassed by the fact that the red suitcase was empty, the journey simply metaphorical. A leap in the dark, Isabelle would have said. You don't have to know where you'll land.

The house was quiet, Isabelle safely asleep. Chloe stepped outside and closed the door, locking it firmly behind her.

IT WAS AL WHO had started the whole thing with the suitcase. That day Chloe had gone to his office, bearing the soup Lillian asked her to bring, she had encountered a man some fifteen years older than her father, with short-cropped dark hair and an awkward pair of glasses that would have told Chloe he was an accountant even if the sign over the door hadn't already declared it. But he had a friendly face and he seemed as befuddled at seeing her as she was at being there—so when he pulled an extra spoon out of his desk drawer, running into the little bathroom to wash it and then handing it to her with a flourish, saying really, she had to share the soup, it was so wonderful—she sat down, without thinking, across the desk from him. It was while they were eating that she spotted the book of rituals.

Al had tried to hide the book at first, but that only made Chloe more curious and he finally tried to explain.

"Rituals are like making time into family," he said. He checked to see if she was following. She wasn't.

"I mean," he continued, and then shook his head, frustrated. "You know, never mind. I'm not very good at this. I'm better with numbers." He reached for the folder next to him.

Chloe watched him, fascinated. Her father always knew what he thought; it was reassuring in a way to see someone, a real grown-up, looking confused.

"No," she said. "Keep going."

"Well . . ." he began, and then he leaned forward, his voice gathering in intensity. "Normally, time just flows along, and you might not pay any more attention to it than you would strangers on the street. A ritual makes you stop and notice. It says, look, you're growing up, or older, or into something. It turns that moment into something you carry with you forever, when otherwise it could have just drifted away."

"Okay," Chloe said.

"And rituals can change you, too," he added. "Make things happen."

"Like what?"

"I don't know; what do you want to have happen?"

Chloe pondered. She hadn't thought about things like that much recently. For the first time in her life, it felt like she was rounding the corner on happy. She was cooking in Lillian's restaurant, no longer bussing tables. She was living with Isabelle, which many would have said was a strange situation for a twenty-year-old girl, and yet the intricacies of life with Isabelle were satisfying in a way she didn't know how to explain. She knew only that Isabelle, with her startling directness, her own lonely places, and even her occasional waywardness, answered a need in her.

And yet. Back when she was bussing tables, Chloe would sometimes see a customer sitting alone in the restaurant, across from an empty place setting. And then the front door would open and someone would enter, and the customer's face would simply illuminate in recognition.

I want someone to look at me like that, Chloe thought.

And then almost immediately, faster even than surprise, she could hear what her father would say about a statement like that, coming from her.

CHLOE'S MOTHER AND FATHER had been teenagers when she was born, no more ready for parenthood than they had been prepared for sex. Chloe's formative years were built upon a framework of cautionary tales in which her own existence was held up as a prime example of the consequences of reckless actions. Chloe's mother, in an act of penance, or perhaps merely in a search for domestic normalcy, had attempted to emulate the June-and-Ward social conventions she had seen on reruns as a young girl, but the ideal had a tendency to wander in disconcerting directions without the frame of a television set to hold it together. It was a bit, Chloe thought later, like being raised by a nun who kept slipping out back for a cigarette break.

Chloe's father had one standard of measurement for a daughter, and Chloe had fallen below the bar early on. She had been fourteen, her body green and unfurling like a fiddlehead fern—arms reaching toward warmth, legs suddenly yearning to wrap around the slim hips of boys who had previously only been playmates.

She had been lying on the couch with one of them, a boy whose name she couldn't even remember now. The house was empty—she had made sure of that at least—her mother and father at work. She and the boy were swimming in the luxury of skin against skin, their eyes open and amazed. But then, of course, as if in a scene she had watched multiple times in movies, she heard her father's footsteps coming down the hall. The boy sat up and yanked down his T-shirt while she grabbed at the buttons of her blouse—but her fingers, which had been so deliciously skillful only moments before, fumbled. In desperation, she had pulled her shirt across her chest, her situation ridiculously obvious even in the dim and wavering light of the television. Her father came in, walked across the room, bent over, and kissed her on the forehead.

He doesn't see, she thought. It's going to be all right. Relief flooded through her. She didn't deserve this kind of mercy, but she would take it.

"Thank you, Chloe," she heard his voice say evenly from above her. "Now I know—wherever I am—you are doing what I knew you were; I don't even have to worry about it. You are exactly what I thought of you." And he turned and walked out of the darkened room.

After that, it didn't really matter what she did.

"SO, what do you want to have happen?" Al repeated.

"I don't know." Chloe shook her head. It was strange to have someone Al's age asking her questions as if the answers mattered. He was listening, and his face looked kind.

"Do you have children?" Chloe asked suddenly.

Al shook his head.

"Dumb question," she said, seeing his face.

"You still haven't answered mine."

Right—like she was going to tell anybody that.

"Too much thinking," she declared, reaching for the book. She closed her eyes and let it fall open on the desk between them.

"I'm not sure that's how you do it," Al said.

Chloe brought down the tip of her finger onto the page.

"That one," she said.

Which is how she ended up on New Year's Eve, with an empty suitcase in her hand, walking around the block to invite adventure into her life.

NOT THAT ANYTHING ADVENTUROUS had happened yet; there was just the sound of her footsteps traveling down Isabelle's front path, the whisper of the old red Samsonite suitcase brushing against her jeans.

"Okay, then," she said to herself. "Once around the block. Here we go."

At the front gate she turned left, away from the Morgans'. The first two houses she passed were dark. The Greenlys were old, likely already in bed; the young couple in the house next to them were just as certainly out on the town. Chloe had watched them move in last fall, wedding presents still in their Crate & Barrel boxes. They had closed the door behind them, presumably to have nonstop post-wedding sex; now the only time she saw them was as they were going to or coming home from work in their matching Audis.

Three doors down lived the Bernhardt family—a full hand of gin rummy if ever there was one, every member seeming to belong to the rest. On her nights off from work, Chloe had often walked around the neighborhood in the evening on the off chance that she might see them through the window, sitting around the dinner table, tossing jokes and stories back and forth like footballs thrown across a backyard. It stunned her every time, the effortlessness of it, as if the habits of a loving family life were something encoded into their DNA.

The family dinners of Chloe's childhood had been different, the main focus being the studied consumption of all four food groups. By the time she was five, Chloe had learned the skill of silence—until she reached adolescence and dinnertime conversations became considerably louder. With Jake, dinners often had been at the grill where Jake was a cook and Chloe had worked for a time as a busser—burgers and fries eaten at the bar after the late shift, when the four food groups tended to morph into vodka, tequila, bourbon, and beer. More rarely, they ate at Jake's apartment, which, even after she had lived there for four months, Chloe never managed to refer to as hers, or theirs.

Mealtime with Isabelle had been a revelation for Chloe. Isabelle had declared early on that she'd had enough conventional dinners in her life. She and Chloe had eaten in every room of the house; they even dined in the middle of the vegetable garden one August evening, Isabelle declaring that they could find everything they needed to eat in their own backyard, proving it by pulling up carrots and snapping off sweet peas and tomatoes, then rinsing them off with the hose. With Isabelle you never quite knew what was going to happen. It felt good to be shaken up like that, although it didn't stop Chloe from taking walks in the evenings.

Tonight every window in the Bernhardt house was fully lit, like in some Rockwellian Advent calendar. A teenager sitting on the kitchen counter talking to the mother who was washing the last of the dishes. Three more kids in the living room, playing cards fanned out in front of their faces, their backs straight and tall with the importance of the grown-up hour. The father upstairs, holding a stuffed rabbit like a puppet, playing a game with a baby Chloe couldn't see.

Really, thought Chloe. It was too much—as if all the bits of happiness of everybody's lousy or simply average families had been siphoned off and given to them. And yet, she couldn't resist watching, the way they always seemed to be embracing each other, even when there was no one nearby. It made Chloe wonder, how much could you hold in your arms if they weren't full of the constantly falling pieces of yourself?

The suitcase bumped against her leg, almost like a dog. She shifted her grip on the handle and continued down the block.

CHLOE HAD FOUND the suitcase in the back of Isabelle's hall closet, underneath a pile of old rain boots. It was red and hard-sided, with metal locks that shut flat across the top with a satisfying snap. Too dated for wheels, reminiscent of a time when stewardesses wore curve-hugging suits and pillbox hats. When Isabelle had seen it, her eyes lit, then saddened.

"That was my escape suitcase," she said. "I got it for my honeymoon. Of course, I didn't call it an escape suitcase back then.

"You take it," she continued. "It needs a spin around the block."

Did everyone think about escaping? Chloe wondered now. Did everyone have their equivalent of a red suitcase, the list in their head of the things they would take if a fire started burning out of control in their family, if the earth shook underneath their marriage? She had spent most of her teenage years in her bedroom, staring at the posters on the wall, the books on her shelves, wondering which of them were essential parts of her, what she would take when she left—always when, never if. In the end, she had taken none of them when she moved in with Jake, so relieved to be away from what felt like the ever-diminishing square footage for her soul in her parents' house that she didn't even pause to make sure there was space for her in her new habitat.

There were places she could stretch into in Isabelle's house, though, and in Lillian's kitchen. And yet, Chloe realized, she still had no idea what she would put in the suitcase in her hand if someone told her she had to pack it. It was a good thing the ritual called for it to be empty.

. . .

AS CHLOE ROUNDED the third side of the block, the Morgans' house came into view once again. She could see the spritzing white lights of sparklers skimming about in the darkness, held in invisible small hands, could hear the laughter of grown-ups well on their way to inebriation. She looked down the street, past the party, to the house where Isabelle slept. Chloe knew how quiet it would be when she arrived. She paused a moment and then turned and headed in the opposite direction, toward the restaurant, her stride lengthening with the familiarity of the route, the suitcase swinging in her right hand. People who saw her might believe she knew where she was going. A young woman, full of purpose and plans, setting off on an adventure.

She was a half-block from Lillian's restaurant, already feeling the happiness that proximity to its kitchen always gave her, when she saw Jake coming out of the sports bar across the street, his black hair curling, his arm casually looped around the shoulder of a new waitress from the grill where he still cooked. Jake's beauty was always a shock—even, or perhaps especially, when he had been hers. He had a way of moving through the world as if he was both caressed and untouched by it at the same time. He paused under the streetlight, his right hand dangling down from the woman's shoulder, just touching her breast. Chloe knew the conversation that was occurring between fingers and nipple—he'd be getting lucky tonight, no question.

And there Chloe was, with hair she hadn't washed in three days and an empty red Samsonite.

"Chloe!" Jake called across the street. Chloe remembered that smile from their last weeks together, the one that had more to do with his own impending cleverness than any joy at seeing her. He crossed the street, bringing the waitress with him. He spotted the suitcase.

"Finally get tired of the old folks' home?" he asked, grinning. "Chloe left me for a crazy old lady," he remarked to the waitress.

"Seriously?" the waitress said, although whether her disbelief was about Chloe's choice of Isabelle or Jake's choice of Chloe was hard to determine.

"I have to go," Chloe said.

"So do we." The waitress smiled, hooking her hand into Jake's belt.

Chloe resisted the desire to make a gagging noise. There was so little dignity left in the situation.

"Hey," Jake said. "Don't worry. You still have forty-five minutes to find someone to kiss you." And then he was gone, the waitress's let's-have-sex perfume trailing behind them.

So far, Chloe decided, this ritual sucked.

She reached the restaurant kitchen door with a relief that quickly turned to concern. The lights were on; she could hear someone moving about inside. Too late for anyone to be there; Lillian had been the first one out of the door for the past week or two, and the rest of the staff should have gone home by now.

A burglar, then? Chloe thought of a stranger's hands touching Lillian's pots and pans, smashing a piece of the beautiful white china, sticking a finger in a crème brûlée. How dare he? Without thinking, she banged open the back door, propelling herself into the kitchen, the red suitcase held in front of her like a shield.

"What the . . . ?"

The new dishwasher, Finnegan, whipped around to face her, and the huge pot he was holding dropped to the floor with a loud thud.

"Shit," he said, bending down to rub his toe. He picked up the pot and stood, his height unfurling until he stopped, erect. He really was tall, Chloe thought, as she watched him effortlessly place the pot back up on the highest shelf.

"I thought you might be a burglar," Chloe said. He still might be, actually—nobody ever used that pot; Lillian just kept it there for good luck. Finnegan held up his empty hands and shrugged.

"As you can see," he said.

"What are you doing here so late?" she asked.

"Cleaning the kitchen for the new year," Finnegan said. "For Lillian."

If anyone was going to make the kitchen feel special for Lillian it should be her, Chloe thought. Finnegan had been working there for just over a month. He'd shown up out of nowhere, the day Pedro cut his hand on a broken water glass in the middle of the lunch rush. They'd needed a dishwasher, desperately, and there, suddenly, was this incredibly tall kid—he couldn't have been more than seventeen or eighteen, for all his height—standing in the rain at the front gate like some kind of waterlogged flamingo. He hadn't said much that day, and even less since.

She stared at him, unsure of what the next step should be.

"Traveling?" Finnegan said finally.

"Oh. No." She set the suitcase down. "It's empty."

"Did you come to—pack food?"

"No. It's just empty."

Finnegan started to turn back to the sink, but he stopped.

"Why?" he asked.

Chloe looked around, as if the kitchen might give her the answer. After the cold outside, the room was warm, heated from the night's cooking and the steam of the dishwater, the air somehow cleansed. It seemed as if Finnegan had touched everything—the black rubber mats were not just rinsed but scoured, the vents above the stove, which always seemed to hold a matte finish of residue, were gleaming. Across the room from her, Finnegan bent forward slightly, the whole long length of his body listening.

Maybe it was the impending stroke of midnight, maybe it was the Bernhardts and all their perfect children, maybe it was the knowledge that Jake had probably been through six girlfriends in the year that she had been living with a seventy-three-year-old woman, or maybe it was something as simple as the urge to answer a suddenly reasonable question—but leaning back against the kitchen counter, the red Samsonite at her feet, Chloe started talking.

She told Finnegan about the first time she'd come to Lillian's restaurant, almost two years before. About the mess she'd made of all her previous jobs, and how Lillian had arrived in her life like a fairy godmother, hiring her as a busser even though she had no rational reason to do so. About how, once she was in Lillian's restaurant, even as she removed the plates and water glasses from the tables, she kept yearning toward the kitchen. The way, as soon as the knives and spatulas, the flour and spices, were in her hands, she felt calm and happy, as if the world was finally speaking in a language she understood.

It seemed odd, Chloe thought as her sentences spiraled out into the kitchen, that she'd never really talked to Finnegan before. Not odd in terms of restaurant protocol—no matter how small or intimate the kitchen, communication between cooks and dishwashers tended to be minimal and perfunctory. But odd in that now that she was doing it, talking to him felt as natural as moving a wooden spoon through a sauce warming on the stove, the way her words would circle out into the room and then back to him, touching base, set forth again by a nod, or a gesture of his hands.

She stopped then, a bit embarrassed at her volubility, realizing she hadn't even answered the question he had asked—but seeing Finnegan's expression, she understood that perhaps he already knew what she was trying to say, probably knew more about her than she thought. Which could have been disconcerting—and yet for some reason when she looked across the room at his face, the way he watched her speak, as if listening intently would shorten the distance between her mouth and his ears, it didn't bother her to realize that he had been paying attention even when she wasn't. She paused, looking at the height of him, the way his hands wrapped loosely around the edge of the sink behind him. She found herself wondering what his fingers would feel like resting on her shoulders, touching the underside of her chin.

Outside there was a sudden burst of commotion—hurrahs and whistles and the sharp crack of fireworks coming from the patrons standing outside the bar across the street, the sound broken only by the silence of sloppy, drunken kisses. Midnight. Finnegan's eyes met hers.

Oh for Christ's sake, Chloe thought to herself, what was she doing? She had promised herself no more restaurant guys, and certainly no teenage dishwashers. She could almost hear Jake joking about cradle-robbing and slumming with the help.

"Lock up, would you?" she said, and made a break for the door.

She raced home and found Isabelle awake in the living room, wondering if war had been declared because there was so much noise in the neighborhood. They'd stayed up for another hour, calming themselves, drinking tea.

"How was the walk around the block?" Isabelle asked.

"Fine."

"And my suitcase? Did it bring you adventure?"

Which was when Chloe remembered she'd left it at the restaurant. Like Cinder-fucking-ella.

THE NEXT DAY, she found the red Samsonite neatly tucked next to her locker at the restaurant. She glared at it as she hung up her coat and put on her chef's apron, cinching it tight in the front before going to work.

The dinner shift was long, everyone worn-out by the previous night's merrymaking, the dining room overflowing with customers from all the restaurants that weren't open on New Year's Day. But Lillian always said that people needed to be taken care of most on January first, and so here they all were. Except Finnegan, who had the night off. Thank heavens, Chloe thought.

"You okay?" Lillian asked as the smell of browning garlic filled the kitchen.

"Shit!" Chloe yanked the sauté pan off the stove. "Sorry."

"Big New Year's?"

"Fine." Lillian was the sort of person you could tell anything to, and most of the time Chloe didn't even need to; Lillian read people the way she did ingredients. Cooking next to her made Chloe feel graceful and smart for the first time in her life. But Lillian liked her kitchen to run smoothly; she encouraged a sense of family among her staff, not romance. "No throwing rennet in the milk," she would say to her new hires. Chloe wasn't about to tell her about Finnegan.

"Did you and Tom do anything to celebrate?" Chloe asked, hoping to shift the focus.

"Celebrate?" Lillian's hand ramped up the speed of her mixing for a moment. "Oh. No—it was pretty quiet."

Chloe cast a quick glance at Lillian. Lillian's life was her restaurant, although she hadn't been there nearly as much recently. Chloe would say love was pulling her out of the kitchen, but Lillian didn't look like a woman in love right now.

"You okay?" Chloe asked.

"Fine," said Lillian. "Let's get that garlic back on track."

At the end of what had felt like the longest dinner shift in history, Chloe took off her apron and picked up the red suitcase in preparation for her walk home. As she carried it down the path to the front gate, she could hear a rustling inside, like dead leaves or a secret. Curious, she set it down and opened the locks. Inside was a blue notebook, like one of those old exam books her mother kept from her single year in college. Chloe saw her name handwritten on the cover. She picked the notebook up and flipped through the pages; they were empty.

CHLOE ARRIVED at the restaurant the next day and walked straight over to where Finnegan stood in front of the sink.

"What is this?" she asked, wielding the notebook in front of his face.

"It's a notebook."

"Why'd you put it in my suitcase?"

"It seemed like you had something to say." He returned studiously to the dishes.

"Right."

Chloe took the notebook back to the changing room and thrust it in her pack. She tied on her apron, kicked off her tennis shoes, and put on her cooking clogs. As she closed her locker, she spotted the corner of the blue notebook sticking up out of her backpack. Chloe shoved it all the way in and zipped the top.

CHLOE AND ISABELLE were walking around the neighborhood between Sunday afternoon rain showers. The streets were black and freshly washed, the air liquid cold, finding its way into collars, behind ears, tightening the fillings in their teeth. Isabelle was wearing the new black merino coat her oldest daughter, Abby, the one in San Francisco, had sent her for Christmas. Chloe had been appalled that Isabelle had spent Christmas without her children, but Isabelle's younger daughter was in Australia and her son was on an archaeological dig in the Southwest. And Abby had her own family now, Isabelle explained. Chloe, who had chosen to spend the holidays with Isabelle rather than go to her parents, who lived only a few miles away, realized she had no right to judge, even as she did.

As they walked, Chloe had to smile at the way Isabelle seemed incapable of talking without using gestures; hands shoved firmly in the pockets of her coat for warmth, she simply resorted to elbows and shoulders for expression. Chloe moved her fingers experimentally within the confines of her own pockets, feeling the rough edges of cookie crumbs, a quarter. A child's life, she thought.

As they passed the Bernhardt house, the front door opened and two of the sons raced out the front door, forgetting to close it as they dashed for the side yard. A smell followed them out into the air, warm and round, onions and garlic, meat and cloves.

"Meat loaf," said Isabelle. "I used to make that."

Chloe inhaled. "That doesn't smell like my mother's meat loaf."

"Let me make it for you," Isabelle said suddenly.

"You do plenty for me," Chloe assured her, but then, seeing Isabelle's face, she added, "That'd be great. Let's go get the ingredients."

The grocery store was brightly lit and full of people, sounds bouncing off the glass panels of the freezer section, ricocheting down aisles lined with cereal and detergent boxes. Chloe could see Isabelle's face tighten, her gaze quickly scanning from right to left. They headed their cart down an aisle lined with tomato sauces and rice and pasta, then walked through the produce section. Isabelle picked up a bouquet of parsley, put it down, slowed as they passed the mushrooms, the tomatoes, and then shook her head. She wandered over to the meat department and stared at the shrink-wrapped rectangles of beef and pork, chicken and ground veal.

"I can't remember," she said finally, her eyes full.

Chloe looked around. "Let's get some coffee," she said. She left the shopping cart in the aisle and walked Isabelle over to the bakery that adjoined the grocery store. They sat at a round table next to a window, looking out at the people running by in the rain that had begun to fall. The bakery was warm, the air filled with the scents of sugar and yeast and chocolate.

"When my kids were little, I always liked to cook on days like this," Isabelle said as she sipped her coffee. "We didn't get this kind of weather much in Southern California, but when we did, I would make meat loaf and mashed potatoes. It was the closest I could get to winter."

Chloe dug around in her backpack and found a pen. Paper, however, was more elusive; the pack was stuffed with old flyers and to-do lists, but all of them already had notes on one if not both sides. Finally, she grabbed the blue notebook and pulled it out.

"Here," she said, opening the notebook and setting it in front of Isabelle, along with the pen. "Close your eyes. See what you remember."

HAMBURGER. PORK. VEAL. WORCHESTER. Crossed out. *Worcestershire sauce.*

"I used to practice spelling that one," Isabelle said with a laugh, opening her eyes. "When my son Rory was little, he thought Worcestershire was where King Arthur's evil older brother lived, and the bottle contained a magic potion. He'd sit under the kitchen table and make up stories while I cooked. I'd hear him acting out the different characters; he thought I couldn't hear him when I was chopping."

Celery, onion, garlic, carrot falling onto the page in a rush of produce. *Bread crumbs*—the letters crunchy, scattered.

Isabelle closed her eyes. Breathed in. *Allspice. Cloves.*

"What a mess I've made of your book," Isabelle said, looking down at the page.

"It's perfect," Chloe said.

. . .

SITTING IN THE KITCHEN, listening to Isabelle hum as she stirred the onions and carrot and celery in a sauté pan, Chloe opened the notebook to a new page.

Chocolate Chip Cookies, she wrote. She remembered the first time she made them, the thrill of the oven knob in her fingers, the sound of the gas lighting, the *whoosh* of heat. She remembered the shiny yellow package of chocolate chips, the red-and-black instructions. Butter and sugar creamy against her tongue, the way the eggs turned the mixture shiny and off-limits to taste-testing. Flour, pillowing into the bowl, rising back up. The smell of the cookies as they melted in the oven and then found their shape.

Her first charred batch, when she went off to play and got distracted. Her second. The time she forgot the salt. The eggs. The baking soda. It seemed she never did it right, her mother's face flat with disappointment as she opened the windows to let out the smell. Which didn't stop Chloe.

"Do we have more?" Isabelle asked, an empty bottle of Worcestershire sauce in her hands.

"I think so," Chloe said, and rose to fetch it.

Standing in the pantry, she looked at the bottles of almond and orange extract, the cans of tuna and soup and diced tomatoes. She could remember putting them in the cart at the grocery store, just in case Isabelle wanted them. She liked to think of Isabelle going into the pantry, finding something she wanted but didn't expect to be there, realizing someone had thought of her.

Chloe stopped. She'd never thought of it before—how, as a child, whenever she had gone to make a batch of cookies, there was always a new package of chocolate chips in the cabinet.

MEMORIES TURNED INTO RECIPES, recipes turned into stories. Chloe found herself filling the pages of the blue notebook after work or in the morning, her egg boiling well past soft as she forgot to turn on the timer, turn off the stove. Isabelle teased her that forgetfulness seemed to be catching, and yet Chloe had never felt more full of memories.

The taste of strawberries, warm from the sun, plucked from their hiding places in the overgrown garden of her grandmother's house, where Chloe would visit for two blissful weeks during the summer. The clomp of the strawberries hitting the bottom of the metal bucket, until the layers deepened and the sound became a muffled plop, while the sun heated her shoulders and the fruit that didn't make it into the pail dissolved in her mouth. Back at the house, she would wash and hull and slice the berries, dropping them in a big blue bowl while her grandmother made shortcake and whipped cream into clouds.

When her grandmother had died, twelve-year-old

Chloe had stolen money from her mother's wallet and gone to the grocery store and bought three huge plastic cartons of strawberries, not caring that it was March and the strawberries came from somewhere almost as far away as her grandmother was now. When Chloe took the first bite, the fruit was so hard and tasteless she truly believed her grandmother had been able to take all of the flavor with her. Chloe hadn't eaten a strawberry since.

But writing about it, she remembered summer afternoons in her grandmother's kitchen, sprinkling sugar over the strawberry slices, the way the smell of the juice came out until the very air around them felt soft. And she thought about what it would be like, a row of strawberries tucked in the midst of Isabelle's carrots and lettuce and tomatoes.

Soon, Chloe started taking the notebook to the restaurant with her. When she had an idea for a new dish, or a thought about an old one, she would write down notes, a word or two that she could develop later. Sometimes she wrote down an ingredient simply for the way the syllables rolled in her mouth. *Chanterelles. Edamame. Mahimahi. Crustacean.*

One day her notebook was still out on the counter when Finnegan arrived. He said nothing, just smiled and went to put on his apron. But the next Monday, when the restaurant was closed, Chloe awoke to a knock at Isabelle's front door. Finnegan was standing there, in jeans and a brown sweatshirt.

"There's somewhere I'd like to take you," he said.

"She'll be ready in five minutes," came Isabelle's voice from behind Chloe's shoulder.

"It's like, what, eight a.m.?" Chloe said.

"I like a man who's an early riser," Isabelle said. "Hello, Finnegan."

"How do you know Finnegan?" Chloe asked.

"I met him the other day, when I came by the restaurant." Isabelle looked at Chloe blandly. "I introduce myself to people; it's a nice thing to do. He's nineteen, by the way."

"Isabelle . . ." Chloe started.

Finnegan turned to Isabelle with an apologetic expression. "It'll take all day," he said.

"I'll be fine, thank you," Isabelle said. "And in any case, Lillian just called and asked me over for dinner."

Isabelle looked at Chloe. "Well, get going," she said. "It looks as if clothing is casual."

FINNEGAN'S CAR WAS OLD, but the heater worked. Chloe lounged in the passenger seat, watching the miles go by on the freeway, lulled into a kind of second sleep by the motion of the car, the sound of the windshield wipers sloughing off the rain that had started to fall.

"Where are we going?" she asked.

"A place my aunt used to take me to," Finnegan said. "It's a ways, but it's worth it."

Remembering her verbal tsunami on New Year's Eve, Chloe determined that she would not be the talker on this journey. It was his turn. She let the silence unfold in the car, curl around the steering wheel, slip through Finnegan's long fingers and stretch out in the backseat. Silence didn't appear to bother Finnegan, the way it did some people, who seemed to think that airtime should be claimed like property. Jake had been that way, always reaching for the conversation as if it was the last slice of pizza in the box and the next meal was uncertain.

But Finnegan appeared content simply to drive, letting the wipers talk their way across the windshield. It was nice to be driven, Chloe thought. Taken care of. Jake had driven, but in a different way, stepping into her opinions and needs and rearranging them into his own. And with Isabelle, Chloe was often the caretaker, a role she enjoyed on the average day, but sometimes it was rather luxurious to be in the passenger seat. You could let your mind wander.

Odd how, when he was in a car, Finnegan seemed even taller than he was standing up. He had to tuck his head to see through the windshield.

"Does it hurt your neck?" she asked. "Having to drive like that?"

"I guess," he said. He paused and Chloe waited, curious to see what might happen.

"You know," he said, "I always wondered how short people did it—reached the pedals and all that. You see those little old women, right up against the steering wheels. It looks like no fun."

Chloe counted to four in her head, imagining a big, empty field waiting for his words. Then, carefully, "What is it like, being tall?"

Finnegan shrugged. "I've always been tall. So mostly, I have to deal with other people not being used to it." He paused again. "If you stand really still and pretend you're a tree, they generally just walk around you."

Chloe almost laughed, and then realized he wasn't joking.

"People say all kinds of things when they forget you're there," Finnegan said.

Chloe thought about all the times she and Lillian had talked while they cooked, never thinking about Finnegan standing at the sink, quiet as leaves growing.

"Where are we going?" she asked again. They had left the highway and were traveling through evergreen trees that made a tunnel of the two-lane road. The rain had softened to a mist, the wipers on the slowest intermittent speed, the windshield gradually filling with drops until, with one smooth motion, the blades cleaned it all away.

"Here," Finnegan said, as he pulled to the side of the road. The wipers clicked off and Chloe saw a brown sign with an arrow pointing to an almost invisible trail.

"Better put on your raincoat," Finnegan said with a grin.

. . .

CHLOE HAD NEVER REALLY been a hiker. Her father had loved it, storming the slopes of mountains and tramping across valleys in his thick, Vibram-soled hiking boots. He would stride ahead, Chloe's mother doubling her pace to follow, while Chloe decelerated in equal proportion, a tactic that was effective when the hike was a straight-in-and-back, but less so on the circular routes.

Chloe's father had always said he could not be expected to adjust his pace to hers, but Finnegan's long legs stayed at her side as they walked the hard-packed dirt trail beside a thin river, his fingers occasionally pointing to the shingled gray bark of a towering lodgepole pine, or the moss-soaked branches of an ancient maple. When they reached a narrow point in the path, he slipped ahead or behind, a movement so effortless that Chloe soon found herself trying it, enjoying the shift in rhythm, the feeling that she was dancing with the path, the trees, with him.

The farther down the trail they got, the more animated Finnegan became, as if being among such tall trees put the world in proportion and made him finally comfortable. They were heading to a waterfall, he said. It was maybe three miles in, but worth it. As they hiked, he told her stories of the animals they weren't seeing, of the rocks around them and the origin of the river. Chloe listened, sorting out fact from imagination until it didn't matter anymore, and they all ran together like the water near their feet.

"What are the trees' stories?" she asked at one point.

"Trees don't have stories," Finnegan replied. "They just listen."

"Do you live with your aunt?" Chloe asked.

"I did. For a while."

"What happened to your parents?" Even as the words hit the air, Chloe wanted them back.

"Stuff."

"I know about stuff," she said.

After a quiet ten minutes, they rounded a bend and Chloe could hear the pounding of water, off in the distance. Had they really gone three miles, she wondered? She looked at Finnegan.

"Come on," he said, eyes bright again, and she speeded up her pace to match his.

The water was massive, surging over the cliff edge a hundred feet above and free-falling in white sheets only to smash on the rocks below, spraying back up in clouds of precipitation. Even from a hundred yards away, Chloe could feel the change in the air, the density of its moisture. The mist reached out and caught in her curls and eyelashes, covering her face, claiming her.

"It's cold!" she exclaimed.

"There's more," he said, grabbing her hand. He took a fork in the trail she hadn't even seen and led her down a narrow path, behind the wall of water.

She had never been anywhere like it. The black rock arched over their heads, creating a cave hidden by a curtain of hammering white water. She stood safe in the darkness, three feet from a force that could snap her bones. The sound was immense, scouring through her, leaving her as weightless as the first breathtaking plunge of a roller coaster.

"This is amazing!" she shouted to Finnegan, and felt the words fly away from her.

He smiled, searching her eyes, and then bent down and kissed her, his back curving like the black rock above them.

THEY STEPPED OUT from the cave and into a world of trees and dirt and trails. The only confirmation they had been anywhere else was the warmth of Finnegan's hand holding hers. Chloe shook the water out of her curls.

"You look like a dog when you do that," Finnegan said, laughing.

Far down the path Chloe saw a pair of hikers approaching. As they got closer, Chloe could hear the man's voice.

"Jesus, I bring you all the way here and all you do is complain about how far you have to hike. I just knew you'd be like that. Ungrateful bitch."

Chloe let go of Finnegan's hand to pass the couple. The woman met her eye, sending her a glance of mute apology.

Why'd she let him do that to her? Chloe thought, as she left the couple behind. Why didn't the woman just push that jerk off the trail into the river?

Chloe kept going, her feet solid on the path. It had started raining again and she pulled up the hood of her coat over her hair.

"Hey, slow up," Finnegan called to her finally. "What's going on?"

"Nothing. Look—let's just say what happened behind the waterfall stays behind the waterfall, okay?"

"What?"

"You know, I bet they were all goo-goo-eyed about each other in the beginning," Chloe said. "I bet he gave her roses and everything."

"Those people? Is that what we're talking about?"

"Yeah."

"You think I'm like him?" Chloe could see the hurt in his eyes. Jake used to do that too, in the beginning. He'd say something awful and then get all sad if she was hurt. Said he didn't mean it, until he stopped bothering with even that.

"Trust me. You'll hurt me; I'll hurt you."

Chloe started hiking again.

Finnegan lengthened his stride and caught up with her. "Okay, look, you're right."

She stared at him, waiting.

"Somewhere along the line, I'll screw up and hurt you," he said. "Everybody does. But that's not the point."

"What's the point?"

"The point is if you believe I would never do it on purpose—and if I believe the same of you. That's how you deal with stuff."

Chloe looked at him, at the water dripping off his hair, the entreaty in his eyes. He did mean it. You could tell. What would it be like to believe, the way he said?

"Okay," she said finally. "Let's just say we're on probation."

They walked up the path, the air holding a quiet truce. The path was too narrow to walk side by side, but Chloe could hear the sound of Finnegan's steps on the trail behind her, steady, matching her pace. When they were almost to the car, he stopped.

"Oh, hell," he said. "I must've put down the water bottle the last time we stopped. I'm gonna run back and get it.

"Here," he said, throwing the car keys to her. "Hop in the car and get warm. I'll be back in a minute."

Chloe watched as he jogged down the path, the loose and easy swing of his limbs, the way he seemed for that moment to be comfortable where he was. She watched until he was out of sight, then she went to the car and took off her sodden coat. She was about to toss it on the backseat, but reconsidered. Better to put it in the trunk, where it wouldn't get everything soaked.

She put the key into the trunk lock and the lid popped open. Inside, she saw a box full of blue notebooks. The top one said "Maridel." Underneath she found "Hannah,"

"Luanne," "Henriette." All the names written in the same handwriting as the "Chloe" on the notebook that Finnegan had given her.

"Well, shit," Chloe said. "That didn't last long, now did it?" She slammed down the trunk lid and threw her wet coat across the backseat.

STILL LIFE *with* ENDIVE

Lillian was a woman in love with a kitchen. It was not the love of an architect, the deep satisfaction in a layout of counters and cabinets designed to make the act of cooking feel effortless. Nor was it the love of a grown-up for the kitchen of her childhood, nostalgia soaked into every surface. Lillian's love for her kitchen was the radiant gratitude of an artist for a space where imagination moves without obstacles, the small, quiet happiness of finding a home, even if the other people in it are passing through—maybe even a bit because of that.

She had built her restaurant kitchen out of scents and tastes and textures, the clean canvas of a round white dinner plate, the firm skins of pears and the generosity of soft cheeses, the many-colored spices sitting in glass jars along the open shelves like a family portrait gallery. She belonged there.

LILLIAN PAUSED OUTSIDE her restaurant kitchen doorway one morning in late February, noting the way winter temperatures could crystallize the olfactory life of a city. Even the aroma coming from the bakery down the street seemed muted, reduced to a gentle reminder of its usual fecundity. Lillian breathed in the air, filling her body with the cold, clear scent of almost-nothing.

"Okay," she said aloud.

She opened the kitchen door and the smells came to greet her. The sensual, come-hither scent of chocolate cake. Mint, for the customer who always liked hers fresh-picked for her late-night tea. Red pepper seeds and onion skins, waiting in the compost pail that Finnegan had not, she could tell, emptied last night. Cooked boar meat from a ragout sauce that was a winter tradition, the smell striding toward her like a strong, sweaty hunter.

"Oh, hell," she muttered, and raced, once again, for the bathroom.

IT WASN'T THE FLU—that possibility had been ruled out a while ago, she thought as she sat on the bathroom floor, resting her forehead against the toilet paper roll that hung on the wall. No fever, no aches, just the roiling in her stomach set off by every smell that was brighter, or heavier, or sweeter or richer or spicier than air. Which didn't leave much.

She should have known, the night it happened. At thirty-six, she was a perfectly viable candidate for procreation and a woman in possession of a fair amount of common sense. But that night in December, everything had been different. She had come home from the restaurant, her neck cricked into a spasm by an ill-timed grab for a pot falling off a shelf. She had gotten into bed on the side that she hoped would be the least painful, grateful for the heat of Tom's body against her, and dropped into sleep.

In the middle of the night, Tom had reached for her. His passion had been so clean, unencumbered, the moment so miraculous and evanescent, that it was hard to believe it was real or anything lasting could come from it, and she had leaned into him without fully waking, letting go. By the end of the next day, she had seen him being pulled back into the ocean of his memories—and when she finally realized what their actions had created, she had no way of telling him.

This was the downside of being involved with a widower. Lillian knew how long it could take for a person to regenerate the heart, the lungs, the sensitive nerves in the fingertips that seemed to go into the ground along with someone you love. She had sensed he was still in the middle of it when he came to the restaurant kitchen door after that last night of the cooking class ten months before and asked her to go for a walk with him. But Lillian had gone anyway, convinced, as she had always been, that somehow food and love could fix anything.

And it had, for the most part. She and Tom had grown toward and into each other, filling spaces left by loss. There had been joy, plenty of it, along with healing. She knew Tom loved her—but she knew as well what it felt like to live with someone whose mind was always partly claimed by the person who wasn't there.

You should have known, Lily, she thought, as she pulled herself up from the restaurant bathroom floor and washed her face. Three was never a number that worked for you.

AS SHE OPENED the bathroom door, Lillian heard someone in the kitchen. It was Monday, the restaurant closed and cooking class between sessions. Lillian had come in herself with the hope of being alone in the space and creating a truce with the aromas of her restaurant, although it was becoming clear that neither of those goals was likely to be achieved that day.

She entered the kitchen and saw Finnegan, holding the compost pail in his hands. He'd been remarkably absentminded recently. She'd noticed the way he and Chloe had been gravitating toward each other, only to bounce away a few weeks ago as if their magnetic fields had been reversed. Now they tended to circle one another in a large orbit, which was problematic in a small kitchen. Usually, Lillian could come up with something to fix the problem, but right now, all she could focus on was what was left of her breakfast.

"I'm sorry," Finnegan said. "I forgot the compost last night. And I know how smells, I mean . . ."

Lillian looked at him.

"Well, you know . . ." He headed outside, where Lillian heard the sound of the compost bin being opened and then closed and latched.

"What did you mean, Finnegan?" she asked as he came back inside and headed toward the sink to rinse out the pail.

"I'm sorry." He was fidgeting, Lillian realized.

"You probably don't want to talk about it yet," Finnegan continued hurriedly. "But I just want you to know . . . I mean, if you need anything or . . ."

Lillian waited.

"The baby," he said finally.

The word hung in the air like a Christmas ornament, gold and gleaming. She hadn't said it out loud yet; somehow it made an odd sort of sense that the first time would come from this tall, gangly young man, his eyes so earnest and full of trepidation. She let the word come toward her, round and full. She could feel the muscles in her jaw relax, a sense of possibility surround her. Finnegan smiled and turned back to the sink, pulling up the bottle of bleach from underneath and pouring some into the pail.

The smell hit her like a freight train.

"SO, what are we going to do?" Finnegan asked, as she came out of the bathroom again.

She looked at Finnegan's inquiring face, then about the kitchen. She was the chef. The teacher. She didn't mind help when it came to chopping vegetables or doing dishes, but this kind was different, and she didn't quite know what to do with it.

"I'm going to the farmers' market," she said. "You should take your day off. I'll see you later."

She went out the kitchen door, and then turned around.

"But thank you," she added.

THE VERY ACT OF PARKING her car near the public market always relaxed Lillian's breathing. She looked at the produce stalls, a row of jewels in a case, the colors more subtle in the winter, a Pantone display consisting only of greens, without the raspberries and plums of summer, the pumpkins of autumn. But if anything, the lack of variation allowed her mind to slow and settle, to see the small differences between the almost-greens and creamy whites of a cabbage and a cauliflower, to wake up the senses that had grown lazy and satisfied with the abundance of the previous eight months. Winter was a chromatic palate-cleanser, and she had always greeted it with the pleasure of a tart lemon sorbet, served in a chilled silver bowl between courses.

She got out of the car and ran for the stalls, head down against the rain that had started to fall. If possible, she liked the market even better in the rain; it dissuaded the tourists, who tended to stay cuddled under the voluminous down comforters of their hotel rooms, leaving the market a private affair, held close under its metal roof, the precipitation providing a sound track part marimba, part moss.

Lillian had her own private routine when it came to the market. She always started by strolling along the aisles, chatting with the farmers she had come to know over the years, nodding politely to the ones she knew were not above sneaking into the Safeway before arriving if their own offerings were unattractive that day. Her eyes would wander over the displays, mentally picking up ingredients and placing them next to each other in her imagination, creating the menu for the evening, her thoughts playing happily, energized and content.

Over the years, she had watched the children who came to her restaurant, noting the ones who sat with gadgets in their hands as they waited for their meals to arrive. She was always a little frustrated by their mental disconnection from their surroundings, but one time she had asked a particularly intent young boy what he was doing, and he showed her a series of shapes tumbling down the screen, orange and green and blue and red, rectangles and squares and ones that looked like straight-edged hats—the boy manipulating them into place, fitting them together so they formed a smooth, even line at the bottom. And she had nodded, understanding the satisfaction in making several different things into one.

While Lillian's childhood friends had had favorite objects—a doll constantly clutched against a prepubescent chest; a plastic horse, caught in mid-stride—Lillian had always been soothed by food. Not the eating of it, although a spoonful of custard could almost always be counted on to set her world to rights. But she had realized early on that it wasn't simply the taste of the custard or the cool curve of a spoon slipping across her tongue, it was the creation of the dish that spoke to her—the careful warming of the milk and the beating of the eggs, the dark mystery of nutmeg, the pouring of the liquid into small, round ramekins that she would set in a shallow bath of water in the oven, the watching as all the parts came together and turned from liquid to solid, gentled white and then just slightly gold.

It was easy for her to combine ingredients and make something new, or to be the teacher placing two students next to each other and watching their flavors bloom in proximity. But in her own life, "we"—that word Finnegan had used with seemingly so little effort back in the kitchen—was a concept laden with complications. There had been a "we" in Lillian's childhood, but she had been, as often as not, circling, not part of, the word—watching her mother reading, always reading, avoiding the fact of the husband who had left when Lillian turned four, a man whose absence was more palpable than the hard wooden chairs in the kitchen, and certainly more so than the books in her mother's hands.

Perhaps that had been one of the things that had drawn her to Tom, Lillian thought as she traveled the aisles of the produce market. She remembered that first walk with him, how at times it had reminded her of when she used to walk home from elementary school with her friends Elizabeth and Mary, the way someone would always have to linger behind or walk ahead in order for them all to fit on the sidewalk, creating a wavering line of three. Lillian had always chosen to fall back, watching the others in front of her. You learned a lot in that position, she'd found, even with Tom.

So, at the end of that first walk with Tom, she'd sent him away, but a month later, when she saw him sitting at a table in her restaurant, she had felt herself pulled across the room. She had thought it was by the essence of him or the desire in his eyes, but now she wondered if what had been so alluring was merely the intimacy of familiarity, a sense of being the first responder to an accident where she already had the necessary skills.

. . .

THE PUBLIC MARKET was quieter on Mondays, particularly rainy ones, and Lillian took her time wandering through the stalls. Acres of spice-covered almonds, blackberry and lavender honey, chocolate-covered cherries, their young saleswoman reaching forward with samples, her low-cut shirt selling more than fruit. The seafood shop, crabs lined up like a medieval armory, fish swimming through a sea of ice. Her ultimate goal was at the end of the aisle—a produce stand staffed by an elderly man who, some people joked, had been at the market since its beginning a hundred years before. George's offerings were the definition of freshness, corn kernels pillowing out of their husks, Japanese eggplant arranged like deep purple parentheses. The tourists didn't like him, because he yelled when they touched the shiny objects he so tantalizingly displayed, but the restaurant owners knew to come to him for the items he kept behind the counter.

"Cooking class tonight?" he asked her as she approached.

"No," she said, "we're between sessions. I just missed your handsome face."

George laughed. His body was crabbed and twisted as old tree roots and the sight of him made Lillian suddenly want to cry with affection. Hormones, she chided herself, stifling the urge.

"I have something for you," he said, and reached

under the counter, pulling out three neat white ovals tipped with the palest of green, a lesson in self-containment in contrast with the blowsy red- and green-leaf lettuce, the sturdiness of the kale and chard arranged across his shelves.

Lillian had grown Belgian endive herself a few times, but the labor involved was extensive. Endive was a plant grown twice—it was started from seeds, but later the plant was dug up, the vegetation cut off, and the root base, dense with energy, replanted and covered so the new growth would stay white. The resulting leaves had a distinctive, slightly bitter taste that could be used for contrast in green salads or braised into sweetness.

For the first time in six weeks, Lillian could feel her body reaching out toward a food, wanting to bring it closer. She took the endive in her hands where they nestled, quiet as eggs.

"Do you want some of the frisée as well?" the produce man asked her, holding it up, its lacey edges cascading over his hand. "A little shallot vinaigrette, a poached egg on top? A perfect Monday night dinner."

"Just a lemon," she said, as she put the endive in her cloth shopping bag. He handed her a lemon, but quickly reached under the counter again and brought out an orange globe, its color almost vibrating in the cool light of the produce stalls.

"Clementine," he said, "for the end of the season."

When Lillian was young, clementines had been a

highlight of winter, the boxes arriving in stores in early December, a gastronomical equivalent of Christmas lights. Expensive, foreign, longed for throughout the rest of the year, they were something to be saved for a special occasion. She could remember the thrill of eating the first one of the season, the way her thumb would slip under the loose peel, pulling it away from the squat, juice-filled fruit inside. She would ration out the box until it was clear that mold would beat her to the rest, and then she would eat one after another until it felt as if summer ran through her veins.

Even now, when you could get clementines at almost any time of year, she restricted herself to the Christmas ones, unwilling to give up the feeling of anticipation, the taste of a fruit utterly in its season. She had stopped buying them a few weeks ago, but this one was perfect, and she took the fruit from him and placed it in her bag.

"You never know when you're going to want a little extra Christmas," George said with a nod.

FINNEGAN MUST HAVE SPENT the whole time she was gone cleaning, Lillian thought as she reentered the restaurant kitchen. The smell of bleach, of compost, even the chocolate from the previous night's cake had been replaced by the clear, bright scent of lemon. He must have chopped up a fresh one and put it down the garbage disposal, she realized, for once not worried about the waste, only glad she had succumbed to the temptation to buy another one at the market. Lemon was one of the few smells she could tolerate these days, and she had bought lemon-scented soap that she kept at home and in the bathroom at the restaurant for when the aromas of cooking grew too overwhelming.

Lillian turned on the oven and laid the yellow lemon, the clementine, and the three white ovals of endive on the wooden chopping block. Her mind had been racing for weeks, thoughts piling on one another like one of those chain-restaurant pizzas with ten ingredients too many. She liked the feel of the minimalist still life in front of her; she wanted a day like that—a few ingredients, an oven, time spent doing nothing.

She pulled out a heavy Dutch oven and collected butter from the walk-in refrigerator. The ingredients in front of her were safe, their smells neutral or clean. With a sharp knife, she carefully chopped off the hard end of the endive, leaving enough of a base to hold the leaves together. She cut the heads in half lengthwise and arranged them in a neat row in the bottom of the pot, their edges brushing against one another like delicately frilled skirts. She cut off small bits of butter, which she scattered over the leaves, finishing off with three generous squeezes of lemon and a few grinds of salt and pepper, adding just a bit of water in the bottom of the pan. She took a piece of parchment paper and ran the end of a cube of butter across it in smooth, straight strokes, watching the surface turn from matte to shine, then laid it across the top of the endive. The heavy cover of the pot settled into place with its usual grumblings, and she placed it in the oven. There.

It would take an hour or so. She could leave, run an errand, take a walk. But instead she brought a chair out of the small break room and sat down next to the oven. The kitchen was warming from its heat; the dining room on the other side of the swinging door was hushed and uninhabited. For this one moment everything was as it used to be. She sat and looked about her.

"We need to talk," she said aloud, into the empty space.

BY THE TIME LILLIAN had turned twelve years old, cooking had become her family. It had taught her lessons usually imparted by parents—economy from a limp head of celery left too long in the hydrator, perseverance from the whipping of heavy cream, the power of memories from oregano, whose flavor only grew stronger as it dried. Her love of new ingredients had brought her to Abuelita, the owner of the local Mexican grocery store, who introduced her to avocados and cilantro, and taught her the magic of matching ingredients with personalities to change a person's mood or a life. But the day when twelve-year-old Lillian had handed her mother an apple—fresh-picked from the orchard down the road on an afternoon when Indian summer gave over to autumn—and Lillian's mother had finally looked up from the book she was reading, food achieved a status for Lillian that was almost mystical.

"Look how you've grown," Lillian's mother had said, and life had started over again. There was conversation at dinner, someone else's hand on the brush as it ran through her hair at night. A trip to New York, where they had discovered a secret fondue restaurant, hidden behind wooden shutters during the day, open by candlelight at night. Excursions to farmers' markets and bakeries and a shop that made its own cheese, stretching and pulling the mozzarella like taffy. Finally, Lillian felt like she was cooking for a mother who was paying attention, and she played in an open field of pearl couscous and Thai basil, paella and spanakopita and eggplant Parmesan. And then one day, two months after Lillian's sixteenth birthday, her mother had collapsed in the grocery store as they were shopping for Sunday dinner. A brain aneurysm, the doctors said. Too many words in her head, Lillian thought. No space left. And Lillian was alone again.

Cooking provided Lillian with homes after that. Abuelita had taken her in and taught her the art of tamales and chiles rellenos in the afternoons when Lillian got home from school, her hands finding solace in the rhythms of stirring and folding. Pierre gave Lillian her first restaurant job as a prep cook at the age of eighteen; three years later, Federico stole her away and raised her status to sous-chef, renting her the apartment above his restaurant for a ridiculously low rate. And all that time she dreamed and planned for the day when she would have her own kitchen, her own customers.

And now, here she was. She had fought for this restaurant, paid her dues—worked until two in the morning for years, demurred to the flashy egos of chefs who knew much and pretended more, just for the chance to watch them reduce a sauce into a moment of perfection. She had received burns and cuts, and, increasingly, compliments. When she was not even thirty, she had gotten the attention that opened the doors of a bank that would lend her money; she had taken over a wreck of a building and turned it into a place where people ate or took classes and remembered, or learned, why they loved each other.

This kitchen was hers. She looked out at the winter light coming in through the windows, listening to the rain-softened sound of the cars on the street. The room was warm, and the gentle scents of the braising endive reached out from the oven, welcoming her back.

She pulled out the Dutch oven and raised its lid. The leaves had melted into glistening layers, the color darker, shining. She took a knife and fork and tentatively cut off a bite. Its texture was silken, but with just the slightest bit of resistance beneath her teeth. The butter melted across her tongue. As she tasted, she thought of her customers, the expressions on their faces as they would eat the dish, the way it would bring them home to themselves. She thought of pairing the endive with a tender pork roast and a green salad with crisp apple slices and tart cranberries and pine nuts, a play off the holidays, like confetti after a party. For dessert, a creamy orange gelato, a bit of sunshine to shift their gaze forward into the coming year.

She smiled as she felt the menu come together, the world making complete and satisfying sense. This world. Her world.

She looked down.

"I can't give this up," she said to the baby inside her.

But even as she said it, she didn't know what that meant.

LILLIAN PUT HER KEY in the front door of Tom's house. She couldn't say "their" house yet, although her things had been casually migrating from her apartment over the past few months. She still kept her place, the one she'd had for fifteen years while Federico, the landlord, had evolved from boss to lover to friend and supporter. She still liked living above the bustle of a restaurant, especially one that wasn't hers, its sounds and smells comforting without demanding her attention.

It was unlikely that Federico would be thrilled about any man impregnating the woman he saw as his culinary protégée. She could just imagine his response if she told him about the baby—the lectures about the hours and dedication it took to run a restaurant.

"Your kitchen is your mistress, your wife, your home," he would tell her, his Italian accent thickening with each word. The fact that he used to tell her this even as they were lying in his bed didn't diminish the impact of the sentiment. She understood what he meant.

No, she couldn't confide in Federico, any more than she could tell Abuelita, who had returned to Mexico a few months ago, and would have had difficulty accepting an unwed pregnancy, no matter how much she loved Lillian. This one was hers to deal with, Lillian thought as she heard her key click in Tom's front-door lock.

Tom's house was empty, although that was to be expected. Tom had been given a high-profile case at the law firm, and these days he left early in the morning, often returning even later at night than she did. While she missed him, it had made it easier to disguise her symptoms. She didn't have to cook for him, either—he ate sandwiches at the office or stepped out for a burger in the evenings before heading back to the office. If she put lemon lotion on her hands and kept them near her face, she could sleep her way through the smell of mustard and grilled meat that still clung to him when he came home.

It hadn't always been this way. In the beginning, Tom had delighted in running away from work—taking Mondays off, coming by for a slow morning in her apartment, listening to Federico singing below as he prepared for the lunch crowd, the smells of ribollita and lasagna sneaking up the stairs. Other days, Tom would leave work early and come by the restaurant, cajoling her into dining with him out at a small table he set up in the garden. Hidden from the customers by the low-hanging branches of the cherry trees, they would eat with their fingers, leaning into each other's words. Afterward, he would wait for her, sitting on a stool in the kitchen and chatting with the staff as they worked.

"You're the mascot," Chloe would say, placing a small origami chef's hat on his head, and they laughed while Chloe made him chop onions for her, although she said he really needed to take a class in knife skills.

And when Lillian would finally lock up the restaurant at the end of the night, she and Tom would walk home through the summer, then autumn, evenings, Tom's arm around her, his hand resting on her shoulder like a promise.

The first time she had gone to his house, it was filled with photographs—Tom and his wife at the beach, Charlie laughing in a bikini, tall and golden and gorgeous. Their honeymoon in Italy. Charlie again, toward the end, with a buzz-cut and hollowed-out cheekbones, somehow more beautiful than in any of the other pictures.

"Is that her?" Lillian asked, already knowing.

"Yes," said Tom. "I'm sorry, I can take them down."

"No," Lillian said. "It's all right."

He did it anyway, photographs disappearing one at a time over the weeks. But people lingered in objects as well as pictures, Lillian found—the smell of perfume in a blue chenille blanket on the couch, a pale green woman's bathrobe hanging in the closet. One time Lillian had opened a bottle of red wine and was reaching for a pair of handblown wineglasses when she caught the expression of horror on Tom's face and quickly pulled her hand back. The next time she came over, the wineglasses were gone. She didn't know where they went, but she doubted somehow it was far.

"I don't mind if you keep things," she told him. She knew what it was like to want to hold on to the smell, the feel of someone else. She still had her mother's pillowcase even though the lavender scent of her mother's night cream was long gone, the fabric now only a caress against her skin.

But Lillian had found even as a child that more complicated than mourning was a jealousy of someone who wasn't there and never would be. Lillian's father had left so early in her life that she had few memories of him, but Lillian's mother saw her husband in the characters of every novel she read, in the place that wasn't set at the table, in the bed where she slept only on the left-hand side, although she still always replaced both pillowcases when she did laundry. When it came to Lillian's mother, her husband was more present in his absence, and Lillian often felt as if she resented him more for the way he had taken her mother away than for his own exit.

And it was even harder with Charlie, who hadn't wanted to leave. Tom's anger, that propulsive emotion that often vaulted humans forward to the next stage, to the next person in their lives, was directed at fate, an emotion that tied him even more strongly to Charlie.

Lillian knew that time was the only real solution for grief, but the loss of her mother had also taught her that unlimited lengths of time were nothing to be counted on. She had spent her childhood waiting for her father to come back, for her mother to stop reading. As an adult, she had waited for someone who could break through her carefully constructed persona of chef and teacher—the culinary generosity that allowed her always to be the giver, the perceptivity that kept her safe from the insights of others. She was so tired of waiting. And by the night of the last cooking class, when Tom had shown up at her back kitchen door, she had begun to suspect that in order to live, sometimes you simply had to leap into the gap left by sorrow, the only hope that you would feel the solid ledge of the other side under your feet as you fell.

Yet in all the scenarios that Lillian had played out in her head, all the ways that things with Tom could go right or wrong, a baby was never part of the landing she had imagined.

LILLIAN'S CELL PHONE RANG, loud in Tom's empty house. She jumped, startled, and picked it up.

"Lillian?" Al said. "Did you forget our appointment?"

It came back to her—the meeting to go over the

figures that Chloe had dropped off weeks before. "Oh Al, I'm so sorry; I'll be there in a flash."

"Okay." She could hear the slight edge of disappointment in his voice.

"I'll bring you something to eat. I promise."

"All right." His voice childlike in its happiness.

LILLIAN HURRIED UP the wooden stairs toward Al's office, carrying a brown to-go box with "Lillian's" written in curling white letters across the top.

"I couldn't do anything fancy," she apologized as she came through the door.

Al lifted the lid off the box, uncovering a turkey and chipotle mayo sandwich with thin-sliced red onions, the crust of the bread dusted with seeds, the top lofting above a garden of fresh lettuce.

"And a pickle," he added, with a smile. "Homemade?"

Lillian nodded.

"Well, then, I accept your apology." He took a white ceramic plate out of a lower desk drawer and arranged the food on it carefully as Lillian settled into the chair across from him. Over the years, they had developed a comfortable routine: for the first twenty minutes of their meeting, they ate and talked about anything but money. After that, they got down to business.

"Not eating today?" Al asked.

"I already did."

Al took a bite.

"Hmmmm . . ." he said. "You're missing a good sandwich." He chewed thoughtfully. "So, what do you think of the idea for Isabelle's party?"

A week or so before, Chloe had told Lillian about Al's interest in rituals, saying she wanted to do one for Isabelle and asking for Lillian's help with the food.

"It won't be a lot of people," Chloe had said. "Just a few friends and family. There's a great ritual honoring elders that we could do for her birthday in March."

Chloe had been moody recently, although honestly, Chloe wasn't the only person in the kitchen with that problem, Lillian thought with chagrin. She was in favor of anything that would shift both their thoughts in a positive direction.

"I like the idea," Lillian told Al as he ate his sandwich.

"There's the food, of course," Al said, "but that throne is going to take some creativity and effort. Do you think we can count on Tom to help out?" He picked up the pickle and the smell jittered across the desk, vinegar and dill and garlic. Lillian leapt for the bathroom.

Al looked at her closely when she returned.

"Pickles," he said reflectively. "When I was a kid, my neighbor Mrs. Cohen used to say you could always tell by how a woman reacted to pickles. If she either couldn't keep her hands off them, or threw up at the smell of them, that's when you knew." He reached into his desk drawer. "Want a mint?"

Lillian took one and chewed.

"So, when are you and Tom getting married?" Al's eyes were dancing. "I bet we could find you a wonderful ceremony." He eagerly reached for the book of rituals on his desk and started thumbing through the pages.

"Here we go," he crowed. "Marriage. There's a whole section."

"Al," Lillian said, "could we just go over the finances?"

"All right. But I'll do a little research for you later, I promise." He marked the section before closing the book.

"In the meantime, could you not say anything to anybody?" Lillian asked. "Even Chloe? Tom doesn't know yet."

Al sent her a quick look. "Of course," he said. "But I know he'll be happy about it. How could he not be? A beautiful woman—who can cook? And a baby? What a perfect life."

LILLIAN SHUT the heavy door of Al's office behind her and started down the wooden stairs, her cook's clogs making a familiar clatter against their hard surface. It had been a good meeting, once they focused on the numbers. The restaurant was doing well; taxes would be about what she had anticipated. Her decision to take on Chloe as a sous-chef had been a smart one and had really saved her in the past few weeks—although she hadn't mentioned that to Al, who had seemed so delighted at the thought of her pregnancy that keeping him on track during their meeting had been like walking a small puppy.

Lillian wondered about Al's own private life. Al's face would grow a little tight whenever he talked about his wife, the elusive Louise, who had never come to the restaurant. Lillian hoped Al was happy, although she didn't really think so. It was one of the reasons she liked to be creative with the lunches she brought, to see the way his face would open as the smells filled his office. She always tried to think of the clients who came after her as well, and fit the lunches to the financial season—more calming scents during tax preparation months, a little more exciting in the summer, when most clients were off on vacation, spending the money Al helped them save the rest of the year. The pickle today might have been a miscalculation, she thought, a bit too much picnic atmosphere just when people should be working hard to meet that April deadline.

Perhaps she should go back up and encourage Al to open a window for a few minutes, she thought. She started to turn and the heel of her clog caught on the tread, throwing her off-balance. She reached out for the handrail, but it was missing, removed by the painters who were coming the next day. She remembered, too late, Al's warning as she left, his reminder that she needed to take good care of herself, his voice full of implied, delighted meaning.

Lillian's arms flailed, catching at nothing, and she slammed down on her tailbone, the air punched out of her lungs in one sharp exhalation. The stairway around her reverberated, stunned into silence. Lillian sat, not breathing, ears straining to hear something that had no sound.

Into that airless moment came a sudden memory of Abuelita, placing her infant grandson in sixteen-year-old Lillian's arms. It was only a few months after Lillian's mother's death and the world was still a raggedly painful place. No matter how comforting Abuelita's kitchen, no matter how many tamales Lillian made, she couldn't get past the feeling that her life was a hole she kept falling into.

"This will help, *niña*," Abuelita had said, and Lillian had felt the baby filling the empty space of her arms, felt its warmth melt something cold and desperate within her. She'd walked about the kitchen for hours, one hand securing the sleeping infant against her chest, the other stirring a soup on the stove or hanging a clean pot on its hook. The rhythms of the kitchen flowed into the sway of her step as she kept the baby sleeping, and she had felt a capacity, a desire to give, rise up and take over loss.

Sitting on Al's hard wooden steps, Lillian held on to her belly with both hands, fingers spread wide across the mound she could barely feel.

"Don't go," she said, with the first, great gulp of air that came into her lungs. "Please please please don't go."

. . .

TEN MINUTES LATER, Lillian cautiously stood up. Her tailbone ached; she would most likely have a heck of a bruise the next day. But it seemed, improbably, miraculously, as if that might be the only repercussion of her fall. She took a slow breath, put a hand on each side of the narrow stairway, and descended one step at a time, placing a clog carefully in the center of each tread.

At the bottom, she opened the door to the street. Out on the sidewalk, the afternoon bustled by. The rain had disappeared and the number of passersby had increased accordingly. A trio of schoolgirls walked in front of the doorway in an uneven line, conversation running up and down between them.

Lillian paused, waiting until they passed.

If she was going to do this, she'd need a little more room on the sidewalk, she thought. And then she stepped forward.

The

THIN WHITE BOX

Louise had been an only child, reluctant to arrive, yanked from her mother's body, leaving behind a footpath of wreckage. Her parents had viewed their new offspring warily. She was an unknown who had entered their lives; they had opened a door expecting a guest and encountered a robber. Even as a baby, Louise could sense the way their eyes skittered off her face, their smell would grow sharp at the edges as they came near her. As she got older, her parents became more adept at covering their feelings, cheering her heartily during kindergarten theatrical performances, posting her report cards, riddled with A's, on the refrigerator, but she knew. Even in kindergarten she could act better than that.

As an adolescent, she discovered a deep reservoir of

resentment that the blame had been laid so unreflectively upon her own infant head. She had not, after all, made herself. It was not her fault that her father had lost his sexual playground and would look elsewhere, not her fault that her mother felt compelled to fill her life with anything that didn't have to do with child-rearing, running off in her nylon stockings and Jackie Kennedy hat to one committee or another. It was perhaps more a sign of the disunion of her parents' marriage that the combination of the two of them would create something that would get stuck, she thought as she lay on her bed, planning how to make her entry into the world of grown-ups something graceful and effortless.

And so she studied those about her, both her peers and those older than she, the ones who already had attained the goal of self-sufficiency and social acceptance. She slept with her hair tightly wound around coffee cans, to straighten the waves that got in one's way in high school hallways. She learned the tilted head-cock of a listener, the silent, nodding encouragement that warmed people into volubility and left them with the impression that she was the most interesting person in the room. She learned not to love science, even though her heart danced in the classrooms where they would watch a mercurial blue dye wind its way up a celery stalk, or a seemingly innocuous white powder mix with a clear liquid to produce a frothing, ecstatic mess. She kept herself slim, shiny, no hard angles that would catch and stall her delivery into the realm of boyfriends, all the while reciting the lines that were like passwords in the secret club of girls—I'm so fat; my parents are driving me crazy; I can't wait to get out of here.

It had been a relief to meet Al, in some ways. That day in the college cafeteria, he had been like a child holding out a broken bowl and asking her to fix it, his eyes so earnest as he explained to her about his fascination with numbers when, in fact, their conversation had had nothing to do with numbers at all. She understood, better than he, what he was asking for. A place to stand still. She could do that; she had been born doing that.

MARRIAGE HAD BEEN a perfectly manageable proposition. Al was a good provider, as he had promised. Accounting was something everyone needed, if not constantly, at least annually, as predictable and obligatory as New Year's resolutions. Between January and late April, she almost never saw him, buried as he was under the stacks of other people's lives.

While the ramifications of the feminist movement exploded and were assimilated around them, Louise was cocooned in the financial security of numbers. There were no children—she and Al had agreed upon that—and she had been left with whole days on her hands, although there was plenty to do, she would explain to her mother, her working friends, the clerk at the grocery store. At first, she had enjoyed learning and performing the multitudinous tasks that made a house and marriage flow smoothly. She had been told more than once that she had a marvelous brain, and she loved to train its laser focus on the questions of which car insurance covered their needs for the least money, or what was the best way to clean the Oriental rugs it had taken her months to find. Her memory was a quick-access storage vault for all the things that would save them money, and she could tell you almost to the hour when the frequent-flyer miles or grocery-store coupons would expire. She was an expert in all things domestic.

Al wasn't any help when it came to these issues. He took an annoyingly blasé attitude to anything that wasn't his own work. He had no idea how much all the small details that she took care of affected the quality of his life, the security of his own finances. He might keep track of the numbers in their bank account, but she was the one who kept the dollars there. She was the one who made sure he had clean shirts in his closet and toilet paper in the bathroom, who stocked the refrigerator with his lactose-free milk, who stood over him while he signed the lines she had highlighted on documents and then made sure they got to the mailbox afterward.

It made her laugh, sometimes, when those telemarketers called in the evening just as she was cooking dinner, and asked for the "head of the household," meaning Al.

Louise was willing to bet that in the vast majority of cases, the person who wore the pants in the family had no idea what size they were. Al was a 34/32.

It could make you rigid. She could see it—the crease between her eyebrows, the contraction at the corner of her eyes and mouth, as if the skin itself was straining to hold in all those details. She wasn't sure why there were so many, but every time she had convinced herself not to worry, Al would go and forget something. Never anything major—she had learned better than to ask that of him, but surely, it wasn't so hard to remember to pick up lightbulbs on the way home from work. He would blink his eyes and tell her it wasn't worth getting worked up about; what was one lightbulb more or less?

She wasn't asking him to do anything momentous, she would fume to herself—it was just a favor, the very smallness of it a chance to notice and acknowledge all the big things that she took care of for him. But he didn't or wouldn't see it, and each time he forgot, she felt the weight of the to-do lists coming down again onto her shoulders. No wonder women got osteoporosis, she would joke with her book-club friends.

But sometimes, when the sunlight came in sideways across her desk in the late afternoon as she sorted through that day's bills, or a slightly opened window brought in the smell of a neighbor's freshly mown lawn, she would stop and simply sit, her mind beautifully, extravagantly empty. And she would wonder what it would be like to have no rugs, no grocery coupons, and fresh, whole milk in a tiny refrigerator.

SHE KNEW AL was having an affair, of course. She had suspected before—the way he would come home smelling of exotic foods that were nothing like the lunches she packed for him, made of carefully chosen ingredients that wouldn't leave those tacky lingering smells in his office. But the suspicions had always been as fleeting as the scents, easily laundered.

This time, however, she knew. She could even point to the day it started—that Saturday morning she had sent him off to the bookstore. He had come back different, delighted in some secret and personal way, and over the weeks she had watched his face widen with satisfaction, had smelled cigarette smoke clinging to his clothes, seen the books he was bringing home. Contemporary fiction, something he had never read before. He even tried to cover his tracks by buying the books from different stores, as if trees could distract her from the forest.

She imagined a young thing—chippies, her mother had called them. Standing behind the bookstore counter, breasts full under a black turtleneck, come-hither eyes waiting behind dark-rimmed glasses. Or maybe thin, anorexic, needy, looking for a father figure. Damaged, in any case—she'd have to be. Louise imagined the two of them lying in bed, reading passages aloud as a prelude to sex. Al could be quite athletic, she acknowledged to herself, when he was in the mood, although he had seemed increasingly to lack inspiration in the past ten years. She couldn't remember the last time he had touched her in a way that could be deemed romantic or creative. She would wait, her body tightening over the course of a day, hoping for something as simple as his hand on her lower back guiding her through a crowd, a feeling of connection that would allow the coils of her life to unwind, but it never came and by nighttime her frustration was burning so strongly she could only lie on her side and close herself around it, warming herself on its heat.

And now here he had gone and found someone else, after almost thirty years of marriage. It fried her, it really did. It wasn't, she realized, that it broke her heart. It was the ungratefulness of it, the lack of respect for her. Why didn't he just tell her? But Al had never been very good at firing people—the woman who cleaned his office was completely useless, but Al felt sorry for her and so kept her on.

Well, she didn't want a sympathy marriage. In her mind, she practiced saying words she had always cringed at before. Bastard. Son of a bitch. Honestly, none of them made much sense, she thought, particularly when it came to Al, whose paternity was well documented—still, the words felt good, the way they filled your mouth, solid as a bite of steak between her teeth. She practiced, waiting for him to come home and tell her he was leaving.

SHE SAW THE BIG BOOK on the seat of his old blue Cadillac when she went out to get the paper one Friday morning in March, almost a year after she had first sent him to the bookstore. *The Book of Rituals and Traditions.* Impossible to disguise, sitting on the passenger seat of the car like a dog waiting for its owner. What was Al doing with a book like that? Louise opened the car door and eased herself inside, putting the tome on her lap. There was a bookmark midway through, and Louise opened to the page. *Marriage*, it said at the top of the section.

So that was it, then, she thought. He was actually going to marry the chippie, someone so special that the usual traditions of white dresses and yellow roses, the procession down the aisle, the rice and the relatives you hated and invited anyway, all those customs she had so unquestioningly accepted twenty-nine years before, were not enough. The chippie needed something new and different. She probably had a name like Morning Glory. Or maybe she was from one of those other-religion countries where they would put a red dot on your forehead or something.

Al was still in the shower and the coffeepot was already started; she had a few minutes. Louise leafed through the pages, looking for clues as to which ceremony they might have chosen, who this girl might be, but there were no indicators.

And then, at the end of the section, her eyes caught on a new heading—*Mayan 52nd Year Ritual*. Her fifty-second birthday was in a few months, adding another year like a brick on an already loaded cart. After fifty, a mile-post that had garnered her congratulations laced with both jubilation and trepidation—you made it! oh dear—it seemed the possibilities for celebration defaulted to decades, a series of signs that you were lasting, then lingering.

So, what was special about fifty-two? She'd never heard anything. She held the book at a slight remove in order to read the smaller print of the description.

THE EXPLANATION of the ritual was brief—all the entries were. It was from Mexico, a chance to restart the clock, as it were. Dishes were broken; lives were changed. She had an image of brightly colored crockery sailing through the air, landing in loud, spectacular pieces, yellow and red and green and blue. She wondered what it would feel like, the cool smooth surface of her plates beneath her fingertips before she sent them flying.

Louise looked down at her watch. Al would be coming downstairs for breakfast: she was out of time. She quickly opened the glove compartment, pulling out the first-aid kit she made sure was always in the car. Never opened—the cellophane wrapping as taut and shiny as when she had purchased it. She dug her finger under the glued-down flaps, cursing the time it took, and finally got to the white plastic box and the tiny set of scissors inside, good for cutting gauze—and, as it turned out, paper. Opening the scissors flat, she sliced her way along the inside of the page, pulling it cleanly away from the book.

Take that, she thought, as she put away the scissors and closed the book again. He wouldn't want that page, anyway. It was unlikely that the new girl would be fifty-two. They never were.

IT WAS JUST A PIECE OF PAPER, folded in the pocket of her bathrobe, but it rustled as she ran back up to the house, the almost-forgotten newspaper in her hand. She was flushed, breathing a bit hard from her quick trip up the driveway. Al looked over at her, one eyebrow cocked.

"Hi," she said quickly. Too quickly, she thought.

"Here's your coffee," she said, pouring a cup and setting it in front of him. The paper made her pocket stick out at a sharp angle; it almost poked him. She walked back to the counter and, with her back to him, pulled the page from her robe and slid it next to a box of Raisin Bran as she pulled the oatmeal tin from the cupboard.

"Hot or cold cereal?" she asked.

"Cold is fine," he said, as he opened the paper. "You don't need to go to the trouble."

Since when did he think about things like that? she wondered. She'd been making him oatmeal for years. He'd never once commented on the extra work it made for her. He was being nice, now that he was leaving. Being nice was probably the chippie's idea—she of the special rituals.

Louise put the oatmeal back in the cupboard, her fingers grazing the page, the contact sending a slight shiver of possibility across her skin.

BREAKFAST WAS OVER; Al had left for the office and Louise sat at his computer in the study, searching for more information. It turned out that the ancient Mayans marked the passage of time using several different calendars that ran parallel to one another—a system so complicated it seemed only Al could love it. Every 18,980 days, or fifty-two years, the sacred and agricultural calendars intersected, an occurrence the Mayans believed could signal the end of the world. Obviously, Louise thought, they had some insight into the realities of middle age.

In preparation for the impending dissolution of the world, pottery was broken—the part of the tradition that had survived to present times. But the ancient Mayans had taken it quite a bit further, apparently. All the fires in their villages were put out, throwing the world into darkness. Pregnant women, who, it was feared, might turn into wild animals, were locked up. Children were pinched so they wouldn't fall asleep and awaken as mice.

And, just in case the world didn't end, there were traditions to welcome the next fifty-two years. A strong young man was sacrificed, his heart ripped from his body as the Pleiades crossed the sky, and a fire was started in the cavity where it had been. From that heart-fire a torch was lit, which was then used to reignite all the fires in the temples and villages. A new beginning.

Louise pulled her gaze away from the computer screen, half expecting to look down and see blood on her hands. She glanced out the window and saw the smoothly paved streets, the yellow and beige houses with their neatly trimmed lawns. She could hear the furnace kick on and felt the warm air whisper across her feet.

She sat in Al's desk chair, imagining a world where women could turn into wild animals. The blackness of a night with all the fires extinguished, all light gone except for the stars. The screams of the young man as the knife dove into his flesh. The visceral intimacy, the intensity of it, stunned her.

When had she ever heard anyone truly scream, unless it was in a movie? Not that she wanted to, of course not, but still, her mind kept circling back whether or not she wanted. She tried to remember the last time she had heard a pure exhalation of human feeling—a howl of sorrow or anger, a moan of pleasure. She knew, without even thinking, that she had never emitted one herself.

She got up and walked into the bathroom, filling her hands with water and bringing them up to her face. As she reached for the towel, her hand brushed against the hair-straightener, and she blindly grasped it before it fell to the tile floor. Then she stopped, eyes closed. She knew what she would see when she opened them again—the smooth blond hair, every white strand carefully plucked out, her nails gentle curves with just a touch of polish, not quite pink, not quite clear.

How long had she been doing this? This house. This man. This wife with the straight blond hair and quiet, unassuming nails, a woman as beige as the world she lived in.

There were plenty of people she could blame, of course, but she knew, even as the water dripped from her face, that she had chosen to be where she was, burrowing into the safe, tidy space Al had offered like a squirrel settling in for the winter.

It struck her as almost funny, in that moment, that she would have hidden herself away for all those years when she was young and healthy and capable, as if the world was most to be feared when mortality was least likely. And yet now, with age so obviously on its way, birthdays stacking up like cordwood, all she wanted to do was take the hair-straightener, bash it through the bathroom window, and run.

Imagine Al's surprise, she thought, coming home, ready to shift the burden of his deception onto her shoulders, only to find that she was already gone.

"SO WHAT ARE YOU going to do?" asked Louise's friend Ellen as they sat in El Beso del Sol eating lunch. Ellen had expressed surprise by the choice of the restaurant—the two women usually ate at a small French bistro with wrought-iron chairs and entrées that peeked out from beneath layers of delicate white sauces. El Beso was large and loud, its patrons drinking what looked like buckets of margaritas even though it was lunchtime and surely they would have places to go afterward.

"I'm not sure." Louise picked up a still-warm tortilla chip from the red plastic basket in the center of the table and dipped it into a small bowl of salsa. The chip crunched under her teeth and the salsa sparked hot and sharp across her tongue.

"Mmmm . . . you should try this," she said to Ellen, motioning toward the basket.

"I'll just wait for my salad."

"There's no point in staying skinny for them; you know that, right?"

"Anger-eating may not be the answer, either." Ellen's smile was just this side of condescending.

Louise considered the chip in her hand, the warmth against her fingertips, the salt she knew would linger there, waiting to be licked off. She had been eating like this for days, as if her body had taken over her brain. Rice pudding, eaten standing at the open refrigerator door, the soft grains of creamy rice dissolving against her tongue. The bright taste of a lemon slice floating in her glass of ice water; the pleasure of a hard pretzel resisting her teeth. The other night she had made hamburgers—half-pound, medium-rare—and could hardly wait to pick hers up and feel the juices drenching the edges of the bun, dripping down the sides of her hands, while Al looked across the table in surprise.

Why had she spent all those years staying skinny for boys she had never cared about, cooking those bland foods Al liked? Whom was she trying to please? Boys who had never intended on staying with her? A husband who was leaving her anyway? Ever since she had read about the Mayan ritual, it was as if a door had been opened to her anger. She had found herself sitting at stoplights, lying in bed at night, resenting all the bites she hadn't taken, longing for all the tastes that had never entered her mouth.

"Are you taking hormones yet?" Ellen asked. "I have a great doctor I could set you up with."

Louise chomped down on her chip and thought about throwing the whole bowl into the air.

IN THE PARKING LOT after lunch, Louise stood by her car, keys in her hand, waving good-bye to Ellen.

Thank God, Louise thought. She had never found Ellen irritating before, but today it was all she could do not to order a second margarita just to make it through lunch. All of a sudden, Ellen's wrinkle-free skin, her encyclopedic knowledge of their friends' activities—things Louise had always regarded with a kind of awe—were deeply and, it felt, permanently uninteresting.

Louise got in her Volvo and turned the key. The engine kicked on and she pressed the accelerator, turning the wheel as she reversed. She heard the crunch and the crackle of plastic even as she remembered the white post just slightly off to the side of her parking spot.

"Damn it," she said. Just what she needed. She got out of the car to inspect the damage: the taillight cover was broken, pieces of red plastic scattered across the ground below the car. The lightbulb inside was smashed.

Terrific.

She got in the car and drove home. At the stoplight at Fourth and Taft, she looked across the street and saw her mechanic's shop. She contemplated going in and making an appointment to get her car fixed, but the light turned green and she continued through the intersection.

. . .

WHEN LOUISE ARRIVED HOME, she sat for a moment in the car, contemplating her house. She thought about what she needed to do inside—laundry moved from the washer to the dryer, dishes unloaded from the dishwasher, Al's shirts to iron. Dinner to make—chicken with white sauce.

No, Louise thought.

She checked her watch. It was only two o'clock; she had plenty of time to take a walk. She got out of the car, ignoring the broken taillight as she set off north, her regular route. The streets were deserted in the early afternoon—the mailman had already come and gone, no mothers hurrying out for carpool. There were a few toddlers living nearby, but Louise figured it was probably naptime; the neighborhood was asleep.

Within a block, she was muttering, the grievances rising out of her, catching on her clenched teeth before pushing their way out into the world. She knew what she looked like—a crazy, childless middle-aged woman walking through the neighborhood talking to herself—but every time she managed to stop, it was only to realize that she had started again, her feet punching time with the words.

Up ahead, near the curve in the road, Louise caught sight of something. A mound. Black, the size of a large dog. She couldn't tell if it was moving or not. As she speeded up her pace, concerned, she heard the sound of a car coming from the other direction. The driver would never see the dog, she realized and she started to run, her purse flapping against her hip, her coat sailing out about her.

She was almost to the dog when the car rounded the curve. It was going to run over the animal, even as she watched. Without thinking, she ran into the road in front of it, her arms above her head.

"No!" The word launched from deep in her throat, harsh and primal and burning. Tires squealed as the car swerved around her.

"Bitch!" the driver yelled at her as he passed. His car continued down the road and was gone.

Louise stood in the street, adrenaline ricocheting through her body, knees shaking, unable to hold her weight. She knelt, and her hand reached behind her toward the dog. She didn't even want to look, didn't want to know if it was dead or close to it. Her hands touched something.

Cloth. Wool. She turned and saw a winter coat, lying in a heap.

Across the street, a door opened and a woman stepped out.

"Are you okay?" she called, concerned.

"I'm fine," Louise said as she pushed herself up to her feet.

. . .

LOUISE WALKED HOME, her throat raw, carrying the coat in her arms. She wasn't exactly sure what she would do with it, but it couldn't stay in the road. Just imagine if a child had seen the dog-coat and dashed out to save it, running closer to the earth, under the sight line of the driver. But a child would have had better vision, Louise chastised herself, a child would have known it wasn't a dog.

The wool was soft and black in her arms. Merino wool, she figured. She stopped and held it out, shook it a bit. A small size, but three-quarter length, which had made for the bulk. A nice coat. What was it doing in the road?

Louise checked inside the collar; she could see a handwritten name on the tag, like her mother used to do to the clothes Louise took to summer camp. She looked closer: "Isabelle Parish."

AS LOUISE DROVE down the street checking addresses, she saw a young woman with curly dark hair come out of a house toward the end of the block. Louise started to call out, just in case, but the girl was too far away. She didn't look like the owner of this coat, anyway, Louise thought, and if it was her house, well, it would be easier just to drop the coat on the front porch. Louise wasn't even sure why she had felt compelled to track down the owner of the coat, except perhaps for that name tag, the handwriting in blue ballpoint ink, so trusting, as if by the simple act of writing a name you could make sure everything would find its way home.

In the end, the address hadn't been that far away from Louise's home—in the same neighborhood, actually, but a part she didn't go to regularly. The number matched a small, white house set back from the street, its garden neatly tended. The same house the young woman had run out of, Louise realized as she went up the walkway. She was folding up the coat to place it on a porch chair when the front door opened.

"Should I know you?" asked an older woman with white hair.

"No," Louise answered and looked up, caught by the inquiry in the woman's eyes. "Here," she said and held the coat forward by way of explanation. "Are you Isabelle?"

"Why did you take my coat?" the woman asked.

"I didn't," Louise said defensively. "I found it in the road. I almost got hit by a car picking it up." She stopped, seeing the confusion on the woman's face.

"Are you okay?" Louise asked.

"That's my coat," said the woman, surprised, taking it into her arms. "Thank you."

"You're welcome." Louise looked at the older woman,

at the blue eyes searching hers. The woman seemed too small even for this coat, Louise thought, as if someone had made a reduced copy of her for the purposes of illustration: older woman.

"I'm Louise," she added, although she wasn't sure why. She didn't think the woman would likely remember.

"Would you like some tea?" the woman asked. "It would be my pleasure."

Louise hesitated. Who knew what this old woman had in her house? Probably cats. Al was allergic to cats; she'd have to wash everything she was wearing. And there was already the laundry that needed to be put in the dryer, and the shirts to iron, dinner to make. And that taillight to fix.

What the hell, Louise thought, and stepped inside.

THE HOUSE WAS SMALL but tidy, and devoid of cats. The furniture reminded Louise of cabins she had been to, clean and rustic. There was a blue-and-white quilt hanging on one wall, a sweatshirt draped over the back of an overstuffed sofa.

"My name is Isabelle," the woman said.

"I know," Louise answered.

The woman cocked her head.

"The tag—in the coat," Louise said. "Isabelle Parish. That's how I found you."

Isabelle rummaged inside the coat and found the tag,

a small smile moving across her face when she saw the writing. "That must have been Chloe," she said.

"Your granddaughter?" Louise thought of the young woman she had seen leaving the house.

"No, she's a friend. She says we're roommates," Isabelle said. "My oldest daughter, Abby, says I'm too old for roommates; she says I should live in one of those homes. I just tell her they are full of lecherous old men."

Isabelle winked, and ushered Louise into the kitchen and motioned toward a chair at a small table set next to a window. The kitchen was tidy; the walls were a friendly yellow, the cupboards and drawers painted blue. On the refrigerator were magnets from various local stores, photo Christmas cards of family groups, and a handwritten sign: DON'T FORGET TO EAT DINNER!

Isabelle took a teakettle and filled it with water, setting it carefully on the stove and turning the dial.

"I used to have gas," she commented. "My daughter says electric is safer."

"Hmmmm," Louise said. A few years before Louise's mother had died, Louise had gone to her house and found the gas burner still lit, the kitchen warmed from its flame. Louise had bought her mother an electric stove the next day.

"But it's not the same," Isabelle continued. "I loved turning on the burner in the morning, that *whoosh* it makes when it lights. It meant the day was starting. Those little things matter. There are only a couple big things left when you get to my age, and you don't mind waiting for those. You know what I mean?"

Louise looked at her, unsure of what to say.

"Ah well," Isabelle said briskly, as she poured hot water into two cups and rummaged about in the drawer next to the stove, pulling out teabags. "So, tell me about you."

Louise always hated that question. Generally, as soon as someone heard she was a stay-at-home wife, not even mother, any follow-on conversation ceased entirely, the questioner departing mentally if not physically. After an encounter like that, she would go home and fill the following days with tasks and plans, new cloth napkins, or a throw rug for the back door, until she would almost forget the look of boredom in the person's eyes. Until, of course, the next time someone asked her.

"I'm a pilot," she heard herself say.

"Good for you," Isabelle responded, and Louise felt the glow of the older woman's approval, even as she realized she had no right to it.

"Did you always want to do that?" Isabelle leaned forward, curious.

Louise paused. What was she doing? She wasn't someone who lied. She'd never made up stories as a child in order to get out of trouble—she'd never even broken her parents' rules, so certain that her birth had used up every coin of familial currency that she had none left to pay off the consequences of misbehavior. And yet, here she was, telling this trusting old woman a complete fabrication.

"Yes," she said. "I always wanted to fly."

Isabelle nodded and set a teacup in front of Louise.

"You know, when I was a child," Isabelle said as she sat down, "I wanted to be a stunt flyer. You know those women who would stand on top of the crop dusters, with their arms flung out and their hair blowing behind them?"

Louise nodded, fascinated, then worried. This could be a slippery slope; soon, she'd have to talk about airplanes as if she knew anything about them. Her mother would say that's what you get for lying. Maybe she should just tell the truth.

"I had children instead," Isabelle added.

"How many?" Louise asked. There it was, right in front of her, the path back to normalcy. Talk about children, recipes, and everything would be as it was before.

"Three. Two girls and a boy. Well, they are grown-up now. They have children, they aren't children." Isabelle's voice mimicked a tone Louise suddenly recognized.

"They come into town every once in a while to make sure I haven't completely lost my mind. Not an unfounded concern, actually."

The sudden, bald flash of honesty in Isabelle's eyes made Louise drop her gaze to the table. What was it about this woman? Louise thought. Talking with her was like driving at night, not knowing where you were going and then, just for a moment, seeing something you recognized better than yourself. It made her feel off-balance.

She took a sip of her tea and glanced about the kitchen.

On the counter, she saw a stack of plates, a collection of wineglasses.

"Are you having a party?" Louise asked, motioning toward the counter.

"Oh." Isabelle smiled, a bit embarrassed. "Chloe wants to throw me a celebration. She calls it a ritual. I keep calling it last rites, but she doesn't think that's funny."

"A ritual?"

"Yes, she keeps talking about honoring elders. That new friend of hers is all about traditions and rituals and things.

"Oh, dear," Isabelle added, glancing at Louise's expression, concerned. "Is your tea cold?"

"Chloe has a boyfriend?"

Isabelle looked confused for a moment. But then she shook her head, clearing it, and continued brightly.

"Well, he's not actually her boyfriend yet. Something seems to be getting in the way, but I'm sure they'll work it out. They're right for each other. She was worried about the age difference at first, but I told her a few years didn't matter. Trust and love are more important, don't you agree?"

"Yes," said Louise grimly. "I certainly do."

LOUISE DROVE HOME in the darkening evening, hands tight on the steering wheel. She could almost hear her mother's voice in her ear, the low, harsh tone she would take on when discussing one of Louise's father's conquests. When Louise was thirteen and her father had finally left them for a woman half his age, Louise's mother had raged for days.

"Men just want the breeders," her mother said, her eyes sharp, but Louise, flush with the assurance of adolescence, had looked at her mother and seen only a woman who thought she could hold a husband with a cocktail of guilt and bitters. Louise would do it differently, she knew, as she felt the first surges of hormones circulating through her bloodstream.

At first it had been exhilarating—she had gone to parties, let herself be pushed up against fake-wood paneling by boys whose jeans-clad crotches moved against her with all the grace of a barn door banging in the wind. She figured out early on what they all wanted—and how to hold it just beyond their reach. She remembered hearing about Freudian theories of envy in high school and actually laughing out loud in class, which earned her a sharp look from the teacher. But really, whom were they kidding? What held more power? The thing that roamed or the home it searched for?

She knew it every time she felt the quick, appraising eyes of men on the street scanning her—up, down—checking the size and weight of her breasts, the width of her hips. Even the ones who didn't seem conscious of their actions still did it—flick, flick—as automatic as blinking.

She had rejected the concept of motherhood and made sure she married a man who agreed with her. She had protected her body from the swelling of pregnancy, the ripping of childbirth. She would visit her friends who had children, their matronly torsos stretched and flabby, and she would return to her home and check her body in the mirror, confirming that her curves were the same as when she first married.

And yet it hadn't done her any good in the end, had it? She'd even seen it coming, really. Al had said he didn't want children, and that had seemed true enough in the first years, when her body was enough for both of them. But after a while, she'd started to notice how Al's eyes would go all soft when he saw a baby, or the way he would smile when there was some story about Little League on the news. She'd figured it was some temporary hormonal malfunction of his, soon to be overtaken by a longing for a little red sports car, but it was obvious that she had underestimated. And now he'd found his own little family-maker.

Louise knew what her mother would say, if she were still alive to say it.

"We're all on the same cattle truck," she would declare to Louise. "No point in thinking you're any different."

And apparently, she wasn't. Even for Al.

A song came on the radio, some teenager singing about love and life and how it would never get her down. Louise turned the knob off with a snap.

. . .

LIGHTS FLASHED BEHIND HER; she heard a quick blurt of a police siren.

It was just getting better and better.

She pulled over, mentally scrolling back through the last few minutes. Had she missed a stop sign? Driven through a school zone too fast? She would fight the school-zone issue; classes had been out for hours. But she smoothed her expression as the young, well-built police officer approached her window.

"What did I do?" she asked, smiling, curious.

"Did you know your taillight is out?" he asked.

Louise looked at him; his eyes held only the simple, official question, his gaze traveling no farther south than her face, and in that moment, she understood what her options were.

Pitiful it was, then.

"Oh, really?" she said, pulling her eyebrows together in concern. "I'm so sorry; I didn't know."

The officer's expression softened slightly. "Yeah—don't worry about it. My mom's the same way; she never knows what's going on with her car. I'll let you go this time; just promise me you'll get it fixed."

Louise nodded, contrite, and the man went back to his cruiser and drove off, passing her car with a cheery wave. She hated him.

. . .

FOR DAYS, Louise staked out Isabelle's house, watching as the level of activity rose. She watched Chloe walking in with bags of groceries; she heard sounds of hammering and saw an extraordinarily tall young man, probably a grandson, carrying a huge chair and paint cans around to the backyard. It was tempting to become curious about the details, but she maintained her vigilance, waiting for what she knew she would see.

And then one day she arrived to see the house empty, but with that resonating feeling of a place recently, fully occupied. Louise, unsure of what to do, unwilling to wait, set off about the neighborhood. As she turned the second corner, she saw an odd parade—a group of ten or so, surrounding something that looked rather like a throne held aloft in the air. She caught up with them, and saw an older woman she recognized as Isabelle, held in the arms of the chair. Below her was Al—and next to him was Chloe, laughing, her face animated with happiness.

"There." Louise heard her mother's voice in her head. "What did I tell you?"

LOUISE HAD WALKED FOR HOURS, her mind whirling, cold and angry. Dinnertime came and went. Finally, her mind slowed enough that her feet headed for home. No one was there.

She unlocked the kitchen door. The key stuck, and she yanked it out with a quick, practiced jerk. She stepped inside and rested against the closed door of her empty house.

So, that was it. The great American swap meet had come to her own life—just like her mother had said it would. She'd given her best years to a man who'd leave her for a child. To make a child.

"Louise, you are an idiot," she said, and flicked on the switch for the light fixture that hung in the center of the room. The bulb gave a quick pop, and went out.

Shaking her head in disbelief, she turned on the recessed ceiling lights over the kitchen counters and opened the cabinet next to her, reaching up to the top shelf where they kept the lightbulbs. There was one box left; as she pulled it down, it collapsed gently beneath her fingers. She stood, looking at the thin white box in her hand, its four openings serenely, pristinely empty.

"Son of a bitch," she said.

SHE DRAGGED A CHAIR across the kitchen to the counter and clambered up, stabilizing herself with a hand on the cabinets. She reached up for the first bulb in the string of recessed fixtures and gave it two quick, firm twists. On the third turn, the heat from the bulb met her fingers and she jerked back, the bulb falling through her hands, cracking on the tile floor in loud, spectacular pieces.

She looked down, shocked. The house seemed to shimmer in the aftermath of the noise. The edges of the broken bulb winked up at her, bright and sparkling, seductive as diamonds. Slowly, Louise smiled.

The next bulb landed hard, the crash loud and spectacular. Then another. When they were all gone, she climbed down, the pieces crackling under the soles of her walking shoes. She went through the living room, the study, the bathroom, emptying every lamp, every fixture. If a room had carpeting, she brought the bulbs back to the kitchen, the pieces crashing into each other on the French ceramic tiles she had spent three months choosing.

When she was done and the house was thoroughly dark, she went to the bedroom, feeling her way through the closet to her suitcase, which she laid open on the bed. She ran her hands over the clothes on the hangers, her fingers recognizing the items for her—the black cocktail dress for anniversaries, the no-wrinkle khakis, the cashmere cardigans which she knew without seeing would be pastels or navy blue. She opened the drawers of her dresser, the smell of her perfume rising up toward her from silk slips, camisoles. She wanted none of it. She felt for the bottom drawer, pulled out two pairs of gardening jeans. Her old college sweatshirt. Her father's smoking jacket that she had found in the trash after he left.

She walked downstairs, the suitcase light in her hand.

In the kitchen she stopped, felt for the pad and pen near the telephone and wrote a note—two words. Then she folded the paper and wrote Al's name on the outside. She left it on the table, picked up her suitcase, and closed the door behind her.

As she approached her car, she saw the broken taillight.

"Just perfect," she said.

Next to her car was Al's old Cadillac, its sleek blue fins rising up like wings. She stood for a moment, contemplating, then went back in the house and found the keys on Al's hook by the back door.

The Cadillac's trunk was huge; her suitcase swam in its vast interior. The seats inside were tan leather, worn from two generations of Al's family. The book of rituals still sat on the passenger seat; Louise picked it up and pitched it over her shoulder into the back, where it landed with a thump in the foot well. With a small, satisfied smile, she put the key in the ignition, watching the numbers of the speedometer illuminate, glowing like a series of new fires.

Those Mayans, she thought—they were locking up the wrong women.

At the street, Louise turned left and let her foot fall heavy onto the accelerator. The car plunged forward, into the dark.

The
THRONE

For the past few days, the world had been hammering and cooking and voices bouncing through the house and yard. When Isabelle's son, Rory, had been young and easily overwhelmed by sounds, she used to tell him to think of noise as the air dancing, pounding out beats with invisible feet. Isabelle hadn't danced in years, but her feet still knew what to do; her arms could still sweep out to just the height of the right shoulder and raised left hand of her boyfriend in college, the one whose name she had forgotten long before she started forgetting things, the one before the man who became her ex-husband—who didn't dance, although he had at their wedding, which she tried to tell him made him a dancer but he would have none of it, none of that, even then.

"Mom!" she heard the voice behind her—within it the clamor of childhood, lips turned purple from sun-warmed blackberries, eyebrows scrunched to better focus on a bug in the backyard. Pink shorts. Bird's-nest blond hair. A distaste for walnuts, melted cheese, grapefruit.

"Mom." Her daughter stood before her. Grown-up, in khaki pants and a soft brown sweater. Isabelle noted with pleasure that her hair was brushed. But then it would be. Abby was a doctor, had been for a while. A pediatrician. So the young man standing next to her might be a patient.

"Mom, you remember Rory," her daughter said. Rory, Isabelle thought, her son—and happiness flooded through her. No, that wasn't right. This wasn't her Rory; he'd already arrived this morning, and he was older than this boy in any case. This was Abby's Rory. Everybody thought it was so cute, naming their children after relatives; they had no idea the trouble it would cause. Unless, of course, you just gave everybody the same name. She'd seen families like that. One Bob after another, until the whole swimming pool was full of them. Bob. Bob. Bob.

"Yes," Isabelle said. "Of course." And she hugged them—Abby's embrace so starched and white that Isabelle checked surreptitiously to make sure Abby wasn't wearing her doctor's coat after all; Rory, tall, with that musky boy smell, holding on longer than she expected, leaving her standing, grateful, her head quiet against his chest.

"You must be Rory." Isabelle heard Chloe's voice coming toward them.

"Is Lucy coming?" Isabelle asked, turning to Abby.

"No, Mom, she's in Australia, remember?" Abby gazed around the living room. "You've sure added some color," she said to Chloe.

"We thought it might be fun," Chloe replied. "Roust out the winter blues, you know?"

Isabelle looked at the orange wall behind her white chair, the big green pillow in its seat. Her cabin on the beach had been almost all white, walls and furniture catching the light that reflected off the water outside until she could hardly detect the difference between inside and out. Nothing to hold on to, even if she had wanted to, which she hadn't at the time. Now that's what she spent all day doing, she thought, the green pillow on the chair as welcome as a homing bacon. Beacon. Homing beacon.

"Has she eaten anything today?" Abby said.

"Isabelle?" Chloe turned to her.

"Why, yes I did," Isabelle answered. Muffins with blueberries exploding warm in her mouth. Coffee, black in a tall white mug, the contrast of colors sharp and beautiful.

"Do you have things in the car?" Chloe asked Abby, looking out toward the street.

"No, we can't stay—I've got a full day of patients tomorrow. We've got a flight out later tonight. But we wanted to be here for Mom's big day," Abby said, reaching out to pat Isabelle's shoulder.

Isabelle looked at Rory; he caught her glance and Isabelle winked. His eyes opened wide in delight.

ISABELLE STOOD IN THE KITCHEN. There were people in the living room; several voices overlapping in their excitement, smashing about on each other like waves. Abby was propped against the refrigerator, talking about something, a car she had when she was in college. Yellow. Small.

"Mom, you remember . . ."

Why, Isabelle wondered, did people say that only when they knew you didn't? Implied inside the words, the concept of volition—you could, if you wanted to. As if wanting had anything to do with it.

A picture popped into Isabelle's mind—Abby's father, holding the back of Abby's bicycle, its training wheels newly removed. "You can do it," he had said, to which she replied with a panicked "No, I can't." He had let go and given her a shove, and Abby, just to prove him wrong, fell loudly to the pavement. For years she had a scar on her knee.

Isabelle walked to the stove, lifting the empty teakettle.

"Let me do that, Mom." Abby took the kettle from her, flicking on the faucet with her elbow. The water poured in, splashing against the inside. While the kettle filled, Abby picked up a sponge and began wiping down the surface of the stove, then the counters nearby.

"So," she said, in time with her sweeping hands, "did you make an appointment with the real estate agent I found for the cabin?"

Isabelle watched her daughter, the speed of her movements. She was like a cartoon character whizzing about, circumnavigating the globe with each swish of her sponge, touching everything.

"No," Isabelle said. "Not yet."

"Mom, it's important." Abby's doctor voice; the kettle landing on the burner.

"I will."

"When?"

From the time Abby was born, it seemed, she always wanted to know when something was going to happen. When Santa Claus would arrive—not just tonight or tomorrow morning, but what hour exactly. When she would begin school. When she would start getting her period. Rory had called her the Portable Planner; even in college, he used to say there was no need for him to carry a calendar when he could just call his big sister and she would tell him where he was supposed to be and when. Which, of course, drove Abby crazy.

"Mom?"

"Yes?"

"When? Give me a date."

In just a moment, Isabelle thought, Abby would say she was going to count to three. One. Two. Three.

The teakettle whistled.

"What kind of tea do you want, Mom?" Abby was standing by the cupboard, one hand on the door.

"Tea?" Isabelle looked at Abby.

CHLOE WAS CALLING EVERYONE into the living room. Isabelle sat in her white chair and watched them come—Abby and the Rorys. Tom from the cooking class. The tall boy, Finnegan, who should be Chloe's boyfriend but wasn't yet, and Al, who had started all this ritual fuss with Chloe, although Isabelle couldn't really say how that had happened.

Isabelle was used to surprises these days, to playing hide-and-seek with the world. She didn't even need to count before words and ideas, faces and memories would scatter off into corners where she couldn't find them. Sometimes they came back; other times they were simply gone. Isabelle liked to think that perhaps some of them had found each other, had struck up friendships and gone out for coffee, or were hidden behind the couch making love. It was better than thinking they were never coming back.

"A couple months ago," Chloe addressed the group, "I started thinking a lot about rituals, thanks to Al here. With Isabelle's birthday coming up, I wanted to do one that would honor this wonderful woman I live with. Al discovered a great ritual, but I want him to explain it."

Al stood up, visibly pleased to be called upon. "Well. The Newar people of Kathmandu believe that the older a person gets, the nearer they are to the gods. The ritual we're going to do today is to help Isabelle get a little bit closer."

Isabelle wasn't quite sure how to take that; it sounded a bit as if they planned to knock her off.

Her son Rory leaned over. "Don't worry, Mom," he said with a smile, "I'll protect you."

Al looked embarrassed. "I wish I could read you the description," he said, "but I left the book in my car. And my car's at home because my wife broke the taillight on her car and I left her mine in case . . ." He gazed around the room as if hoping its walls might stop his words.

Lillian stepped forward from her position in the kitchen doorway.

"So," she said, "Al and Chloe have a little adventure planned for later, but some of you have traveled a long way to get here, so we thought we'd reverse tradition and celebrate first by eating. There are plates and food on the sideboard. Go make yourselves at home and then find a seat at the table."

Isabelle looked about. She could smell the food. For the past several mornings, Chloe and Lillian had cooked in Isabelle's kitchen before they went to the restaurant. Isabelle had sat in a chair at the table, chopping orange scepters of carrots, buttering pans, whatever they handed her to do. She had watched the two women, their words and motions weaving into one another. They had said it was Isabelle's job to entertain them, and she told them stories from her childhood, of summers at the cabin with her parents and brothers, August unrolling in front of her, sun-splashed and endless. Stories of her children when they were small, their round little bodies barely containing their personalities, which bloomed and glittered and melted into her. Of her life after they all left—children and husband going off in search of new and exciting lives—and she had circled back to the cabin to find her own.

It had surprised her, how quickly the memories surfaced in the warmth of the kitchen, how clear and comforting they were. She hoped at times that the celebration, as Chloe called it, would simply be a succession of mornings in the kitchen.

GRANDSON RORY CAME TOWARD Isabelle's place at the table, bearing two plates of food.

"Mom said you'd like this," he said, setting one at her place.

Isabelle looked down at a small mound of undressed green lettuce, a slice of chicken with the sauce carefully removed. She had seen the sideboard, overflowing with the dishes Lillian and Chloe had created over the last three days—chicken in orange-and-garlic sauce, arugula with little rounds of goat cheese marinated in olive oil and lemon zest. Fresh focaccia sprinkled with large, white grains of salt. For dessert, her favorite, warm banana-and-chocolate bread pudding with crème anglaise. How could anyone, faced with those options, manage to come up with such a boring plate of food? It was impressive, almost.

Rory's plate, in contrast, was stacked like a farmhand's, with generous portions from every dish covering the round white surface.

"Want mine?" he asked, looking at her expression.

She nodded.

He laughed in response. "Okay, but if we get caught, I'm going to say you took it."

"You can just say I didn't know what I was doing."

They surreptitiously swapped plates and Rory took hers to the kitchen, from which he exited a few moments later, empty-handed, and got back in line.

While she waited for the others to come to the table, Isabelle took a bite of the bread pudding. It melted across her tongue. Then she tried the goat cheese on a thin slice of toasted bread, and the chicken, citrus bouncing off the garlic. Backward meal, she thought with pleasure.

Rory returned, settling down next to her.

"Better?" he asked.

"Yes, thank you." They ate in companionable silence.

"Rory," Isabelle said after a moment, "I am sorry I didn't know who you were before."

"I grow really fast," he said easily. Letting her off the hook. She could almost feel it pull out, the luxury of wide, open water to swim into, away.

"Ah . . ." She yanked her thoughts back. This was her grandson. Rory.

His gaze met hers. "What's it like?" he asked.

"This?" She pointed to her head.

"Yeah."

Funny you should ask, her mother used to say. But it was true, because nobody ever really did. They did the not-asking thing—saying how bad their own memories were getting, how they couldn't remember a word or their Social Security number—looking, really, for a comparison that would help them feel better, or an assurance that they wouldn't soon have to take care of an old lady with no mind. But nobody ever really asked. Not even the doctors. Sometimes it seemed as if the only real conversation she had these days was with the disease itself, and that one never seemed to cease.

"It's kind of like an attic," she said to Rory. "It has all your stuff but somebody else keeps throwing empty boxes and blankets on top of it, so you can't always find what you're looking for."

Rory nodded. He had one of those closets, Isabelle could tell. Like her Rory's, when he was younger. Full to the brim.

"Is it scary?" Wanting to know.

"Yes."

She shouldn't have said it, maybe; he was still a teenager and he didn't need the world surrounding him quite that closely. Abby wouldn't appreciate it. But the word sat in the air, and in the clarity of its honesty she felt like herself for the first time in a long time. Hello you, she thought. There you are.

HER SON RORY ROSE from his seat, raising a wineglass.

"I think the occasion deserves some stories," he said.

"And you'll start," Isabelle added with a smile. It had been the way he had stalled every night as a child, while she sat by his bed. "I think the occasion deserves a story," he would say, knowing the wording would catch her up, make the day fall away from her.

"I remember one time with Mom," Rory said, looking affectionately at Isabelle. "There was a summer when we were at the cabin, just you and me. I guess I was five or so and you said I was brave enough to see something special. You took me to the edge of the water, and you lifted up one of the rocks. There was a little pool of water underneath and in it there were these two horrible fish-creatures, with these mean, awful faces."

Rory sent his gaze out across the table. "She told me they were dogfishes," he continued, "and if we were very quiet we might hear them bark. She said they weren't angry; they were just scared. If I wanted, I could be their protector, and they would think I was magic. I remember taking the rock and putting it back in place, so carefully, because I was the King of the Dogfish."

Isabelle remembered the sunshine heating the rocks that would, when the tide came back in, warm the water. Rory next to her, always wanting to reach out and touch everything, know the story behind it. The pride on his face when the rock covered the fish once again.

It was Rory who had come and helped her fix up the cabin after the divorce. He had been in college then, and he arrived with the beginning of summer, eyes wide at the sight of his mother with a hammer in her hand. They fixed the roof, rebuilt the porch steps, ate dinners with their hands while sitting on a driftwood log on the beach, letting the crumbs fall to the rocks where the birds would find them later. They had talked late into the evenings, and the separate languages of mother and child shifted into a vocabulary they could hold in common. Even after he left in the fall she still felt him there.

From across the table, Chloe stood up.

"There was one night. Not my best," she said to Isabelle with a small shrug. "I'd left my boyfriend and it was ten o'clock at night and I didn't know where to go. I'd taken you home one time after Lillian's cooking class; we sat in the car and talked and you'd said I was always welcome at your house. I wasn't really sure if you meant it, but I drove by that night anyway. And I saw you, out in the garden with a headlamp." Chloe laughed. "It was January, and it was freaking cold, but there you were, all bundled up, covering your roses against the freeze. You took me inside and made me tea. And here I am." Chloe sat down and reached her hand across to Isabelle. Isabelle could feel Abby's body straightening at the other end of the table.

It was interesting, Isabelle thought, the children that chose you. Some came through your body; others came in cars in the middle of the night. Sometimes it seemed as if the ones who had their own transportation were easier.

"Sweet girl," Isabelle said, and tightened her fingers around Chloe's.

Abby wiped her mouth with her napkin and addressed the group.

"I've thought a lot about my memories of my mother this week," she said. "About how she used to bake brownies at ten in the morning, or the way she would make one dinner for us kids and then a grown-up one for Dad when he came home late. I used to sneak downstairs when we were supposed to be asleep and listen to them eating together."

"I know," Isabelle said.

Disconcerted, Abby stopped and looked at her mother for a moment.

"But," she continued, "I decided my clearest memory of my mother is the time she came to visit me after she sold our house. It was the first time I can remember seeing her look truly happy."

Abby had grown subtler over the years, Isabelle

noted—but then again, Isabelle had never discouraged her daughter's defiant streak, even though defiance could come perilously close to petulance at times. But when Abby was born and Isabelle had seen the fireworks of intelligence in her baby's eyes, Isabelle knew that more than anything, she wanted for her daughter to have her own life—to draw her own lines. The problem was, Isabelle realized, she had always thought she would be inside them, which hadn't been the case at all.

But she couldn't have been inside them, could she? Shouldn't have even thought that—if she was the thing her daughter wasn't supposed to be. The anti-example, held at arm's length. The only hope was that the nearsightedness that came with age would eventually cause Abby to pull things closer to her again. It appeared, however, that Isabelle might be growing older faster than Abby.

"Chocolate?"

Isabelle heard young Rory's voice next to her. She looked over and saw a round, cinnamon-dusted truffle in his outstretched hand.

"THANKS, that was really helpful."

Walking by the partially opened bedroom door, Isabelle could hear her daughter's voice inside, talking to someone. Not happy.

"What do you mean?" The second voice lower, tired. Rory. Her Rory. Isabelle stopped.

"Come on, Rory—King of the Dogfish? Jesus. It's hard enough to get her to think about selling that cabin without you waxing all nostalgic."

"Maybe I don't think that's the answer."

"Really? And just where is the money for long-term care going to come from? She's heading into stage two; if you just looked, you'd see it. She almost never talks—she didn't even know her own grandchild today."

"Maybe she doesn't want to sell the cabin." Rory's voice lowering another notch. Isabelle knew that tone—the reasonableness that was merely covering the sound of her son's heels digging in. She had an image of five-year-old Rory at the local swimming pool, not wanting to go home, gazing at his red sandals as if he had completely forgotten how to put them on.

"I don't know why not. She didn't have any trouble selling the house."

"Christ, Abby, when are you going to let that go? You were in college."

"Medical school."

"My point exactly. It's not like she sold the house out from under your toddler ass."

"But it was *our* house."

"Dad *left* her, remember? We did too, for that matter. Was she supposed to stay there just in case you wanted to drop in? I mean, how many times a year do you visit her, Abby? When was the last time she saw Rory? No wonder she didn't recognize him."

"I've got a practice to take care of." Abby's porcupine voice. "And my son's in high school, he's got things to do. Besides—I don't want him to see her like this."

"Because it's going to get better?"

Isabelle stood by the door, listening to her children talking. As if they were her parents. She had a sudden vision of Abby as a toddler, furious at the limitations her age put upon her, at the way her mother treated her like a child. And now here they were, reversed.

Isabelle had done a lot more reading about the disease that had taken up residence in her brain than the pamphlets her daughter had given her. She knew what she could expect, the slow unraveling of her life. She had walked a labyrinth once in England, on her honeymoon, more than fifty years ago. Her feet had followed the lines that led her back and forth, back and forth, seemingly endless, until she reached the center—and realized she would, after a moment's pause, start the whole process again going out instead of in.

The hardest part, in the end, was the knowing. Knowing that she would change places with her children, lose every skill she had ever acquired. She would give up buttons. Forks. Taking a walk alone. The words of all the books she had read, slipping from her mind while she slept or ate breakfast or went to answer the front door.

She had heard that Medicare would cover hospice only when you were reduced to five words. How long would it take, she wondered, to follow the labyrinth all the way out to wordlessness? What would the last five be? And the sixth?

She had read that someday she would no longer recognize her children, and the prospect was almost beyond comprehension. She couldn't imagine how far her life would have to unravel before they would leave it, she would leave them.

And yet, Isabelle thought as she listened to her children, there were times these days when it might be easier if she didn't know who they were. If she heard their words as those of strangers.

"ISABELLE."

Isabelle turned to see Lillian standing behind her.

"Could you help me in the kitchen?" Lillian asked, and Isabelle nodded.

The kitchen was blissfully quiet, the counters covered with the aftermath of eating. Lillian turned on the water in the sink, added some dish soap, and began carrying over plates and serving spoons, cups and bowls. Isabelle picked up a sponge and began washing, placing the clean dishes in the drainer. They didn't talk, the only sounds the splash of the water, the muffled clink of glass against ceramic as one object settled against another under the surface of bubbles. It felt good to hold things in her hands, Isabelle thought. The water was warm. She knew what she was doing, and relief washed through her body.

Out of the soapy water, Isabelle pulled a bowl, white with blue flowers trailing along the rim. She was surprised. She hadn't seen it in years; someone must have dug back deep in the cabinets, or in the top of a closet. The bowl had a habit of disappearing, and returning when you least expected it.

Isabelle had seen it for the first time when she took her three small children to her family's cabin, for what she had hoped would become an annual summer tradition. Isabelle's father had died soon after Rory was born, and Isabelle's brothers, who lived on the East Coast by then, had said they had no particular use for the cabin, an attitude Isabelle's husband, Edward, had shared. But Isabelle remembered the way summer at the cabin had marked the forward movement of her childhood, the photographs her parents had taken over all those years—children's ages determined later by swimsuits, haircuts, heights relative to the railing of the big front porch that the children loved even as its boards left splinters in their feet. Isabelle wanted the cabin, and finally Edward had relented.

The bowl hadn't been part of the cabin when Isabelle was a child, but there it was when she arrived with her children—on the center of the table, empty, ready for fat clusters of purple grapes, a child's collection of wishing rocks—or, as it turned out, everything.

"That's *my* bowl!" seven-year-old Abby had declared joyfully and so it was. No matter that it was the size of a fruit bowl, not meant for daily, individual use; no matter that a child-sized portion of Cheerios appeared dwarfed, huddling at the bottom of the bowl like starvation rations, leading to daily arguments regarding just how full a bowl should be. Abby argued passionately about the perfection of a bowl filled halfway to the rim and no more, about the benefit of extra milk-soaked Cheerios—if there were any, and there wouldn't be, but just in case, they could surely be put to good use with the stray cat that Abby had spotted as they unloaded the car and which would surely come to love them if only they fed it.

The bowl had stayed with Abby that whole August. It was a perfect mold to create the base of sand castles; a giant sand dollar could fit in its base without a centimeter to spare. If you didn't need it for eating soup at lunch, it could remain outside all day—an impromptu pond that just might attract never-before-seen insects.

When they arrived the next August, the bowl had mysteriously disappeared. Abby and Isabelle looked through all the cupboards, and Abby sulked for two days, until new people showed up at the cabin down the road, with an eight-year-old girl who became Abby's best friend for the rest of the summer.

One day, as Isabelle sat on the beach building a rock castle with Rory and Lucy, she overheard Abby talking with her friend.

"You know," Abby explained, "that the waves come far up the beach at night, right? Well, one night, a little girl left a beautiful white bowl on the beach, and a wave came up and carried it far away. It looked just like a moon floating in the middle of the ocean. But only the moon knows where it went, because only the moon can see itself in the water." And Isabelle—who had heard the magic leaving her daughter's imagination as she grew determinedly toward adulthood—listened, as if to the last clear notes of a radio station that would soon be out of frequency range.

In the end, the cabin had been a family tradition for just a few years. Edward claimed he couldn't take that much time off in the summer; Abby declared she wanted to go to horse camp and Lucy, not to be left out, clamored to go, too. For the three summers after that it was just Isabelle and Rory, until Rory discovered soccer and the cabin became only an annual argument with Edward, when it was time to pay the property taxes.

After the divorce, after the family home had been sold, Isabelle had come back to the cabin. When she arrived, not even certain why she was there, shocked at the state of disrepair it had fallen into, she saw the bowl sitting in the middle of the table. And everything was all right, after all.

Astonishing how many recollections could be held inside one bowl, Isabelle thought, her hands in the warm dishwater. Things could be that way—a bowl, a photo, the smell of anise or talcum powder—holding memories, as if her mind, knowing it couldn't possibly contain everything, had packed them elsewhere for safekeeping. There were days she would walk through her house, looking at one object after another, checking to see if a story was waiting inside. Minds, however, Isabelle had realized, were far more like squirrels—constantly forgetting where they had hidden what would keep them alive through the winter. Still, it was a small miracle these days to happen upon a secret cache and feel memories open up before her, clear and vivid, as solid in her hand as the object they came from.

Isabelle turned to tell Lillian, and there, suddenly, she saw something she remembered in the new softness in Lillian's face, the look—part hopeful, part sad—in her eyes. Isabelle recalled the visit to her own doctor's office so many years ago, his pronouncement, his eyes watching for her reaction while she did her best to produce an expression of elation or even pleasure while inside her mind was racing—how do I do this, I don't know how to do this, I'm not ready to be a mother. It wasn't until the second baby that she had been able to greet the news with unrestricted joy.

"Ahhh . . ." Isabelle said. She put a hand on Lillian's stomach.

Lillian's eyes filled with surprise, then tears.

There was a noise at the kitchen door. The two women turned, Isabelle's wet handprint still visible on Lillian's shirt, and they saw Tom standing in the doorway, confusion and then knowledge splashed across his face. Before he could speak, Abby passed him, coming into the kitchen.

"Mom, you're the guest of honor—you shouldn't be cleaning up!" She swooped the bowl from her mother's hand and set it in the drainer.

"Now, scoot," she said, "out to your guests."

CHLOE WAS CLAPPING her hands to call the group to attention.

"Okay," she said. "It's time for an adventure. Follow me, everybody." And Chloe led the way out the back door.

As she walked onto the back porch, Isabelle looked out toward her garden. In front of it stood an object—but what would you call it? Isabelle wondered. A throne on rails? She had seen pictures of things like that in books, the seated people looking like royalty, or, at the very least, rich and powerful.

But Isabelle had to smile at how utterly different the throne-thing before her was from others she had seen, which had looked more like intricately decorated boxes enclosing their occupants in curtains and mystery. This chair was open to the sky, strong and tall. And decorated. Good heavens, it was decorated. Painted blue waves rolled up its legs, clouds rose up the back and disappeared off the top rail. The vertical back supports had been turned into two pine trees, reaching for the sky, while blue and green and silver streamers fluttered from the tops. The rails that ran underneath the chair were painted with images of geese, their necks outstretched, wings wide.

"There are two steps to the ritual," Chloe was explaining. "Isabelle, if you could take your seat."

Chloe walked Isabelle over to the throne, where Isabelle lifted herself onto her toes for height and then sat on its brightly painted seat, her feet swinging slightly above the ground. Like a child, she thought. All she needed was balloons.

Lillian arrived, carrying the white bowl, which she set at Isabelle's feet. Isabelle could see the blue flowers along the rim, something white inside. Milk? A lot of milk. Too much for Cheerios, that was certain.

"Now," Chloe explained, "one of the most important parts of this ritual is caring for our elders." She reached forward and undid the Velcro closings of Isabelle's purple tennis shoes. Isabelle recalled learning how to tie her shoes—her father, bending over her laces, telling her the story of the bunny running around the tree and going down the hole. She could still smell the blue scent of his aftershave, the starch in his white Sunday shirt. She could remember her own hands, years later, this time teaching her children, their faces looking up at her as if she was a magician as she pulled the loops tight. How could she still see her hands moving through time and space, every detail sharp and clear as an instructional video, and yet not be able to do the action itself? She wanted to cry with the frustration of it.

She and Chloe had bought the purple shoes a few months ago, after Chloe had come home to find Isabelle sitting in her white chair, her fingers cramped from trying to tie her laces. Chloe had taken Isabelle on a shopping trip and they had both bought tennis shoes with Velcro closings, Chloe laughing and telling Isabelle they were built for speed now. Which was nice of her, of course, and for the most part Isabelle appreciated Chloe's tact, but sometimes it felt like covering a broken chair with new upholstery.

Chloe removed Isabelle's shoes and socks, leaving Isabelle's feet naked in the afternoon light. The veins stood out, the bones of her toes visible through the skin like the ridges of a topographical map. It astonished Isabelle, every time she saw them now. Over the years, she had gotten used to her hands, the way aging seemed to move over them like a tide, loosening skin, expanding knuckles. But feet hid, coming out only rarely and then usually in a rush to bed. There was a time when her feet had been plump, ripe, her toenails red (what was the name of the color? she couldn't remember), just a bit of the big toe flirting out through the opening in her black pumps, catching Edward's eye at a college dance. He hadn't danced with her then, but he had watched her, his eyes a source of gravity coming across the room until it took a conscious effort not to look past her partner and meet his gaze, which asked for—what? She hadn't known exactly, which made it all the more attractive. He was so certain, there had seemed to be no need for her to know.

She started to tell all this to Chloe, but as Chloe lowered Isabelle's right foot into the bowl, the thoughts slipped out of her mind, replaced by the sheer luxury of hands on her skin, the milk cool, softer than water, thicker. Her own milk had been thick, rich. One time, when she had been nursing Abby, she had put some in a glass and tried it herself, although she had never told anyone. It astonished her, what she had created.

Chloe's hands moved gently over the knobs and arches of Isabelle's feet, the moons of her toenails. Canary red. That had been the color.

"Now," said Chloe, toweling Isabelle's feet dry and sliding on a pair of soft, new socks. "Everybody ready?" The Rorys and Al and Finnegan came forward, each standing next to one end of the throne rails.

"Um, I don't think so," Chloe remarked dryly as she looked over at Finnegan's towering height. "Lopsided."

"I've got it," Abby said, stepping in. "I think I can carry my own mother."

Finnegan moved out of position, taking a place next to Isabelle, who reached over and patted his arm.

"Don't you worry," she said. Chloe sent them a look.

"One, two, three," said Al, and the throne went up into the air, making its way around the garden, through the gate, and out, into the neighborhood.

ISABELLE RODE ON HER THRONE holding on to its arms, feeling the jostling of the chair settle into a more predictable gait as the carriers adjusted their strides to each other. As she grew more comfortable with the motion, she looked about her, astonished to be seeing the world from such a new perspective. She had thought she was done with all that. Over her life she had grown taller, and then, more recently, shorter. But this was different, a sudden stretch to an unexpected elevation. Suddenly she was seeing the buds on the cherry trees around her; she could feel the energy packed within them, a bouquet of fireworks whose fuse had already been lit. She could smell them, too, a subtle essence of pink and lollipops, the sweetness deepened by the scent of the slowly warming earth below them.

She looked over at Finnegan, who was walking near to her, their eyes at almost equal heights.

"Welcome to my world," he said with a grin.

As they walked down the street, neighbors came out of their houses to watch the procession, the grown-ups making comments quietly to each other. Children called to her, delighted, asking for a turn, wanting to be where she was. She looked at them, awed. They moved through the world and moments spun around them, light as dandelion seeds. Some stuck, some didn't, and they had yet to learn to care. Isabelle thought it deeply unfair that you could start to lose your memories without also losing that desire to keep them. Although that, of course, was coming too.

It struck her sometimes, the effort it took for her to keep holding hands with the present. At times it felt as if her mind simply unhinged—an image of her mother's flowerbed mingling with the blue eyes of the grocery clerk in front of her, a sudden, undirected feeling of lust running through her as she stood in the shower. Sometimes it took a while before she realized she had been gone. She wondered in those moments how long it would be before the hinge on her mind would simply stay open.

It wasn't so much the occasional mingling of past and present that was the problem as it was the unyielding anxiety that she was not doing what was expected of her, the drag of the now-world with its requirements to follow the cluttered trail of a conversation, or put a milk carton back in the refrigerator. It reminded her, in an odd way, of those days when she was younger, married, when she would put on stockings and make Edward's dinner when all she really wanted was to place her hands into the children's paints and feel the cool moisture slipping between her fingers, the resistance of the thick brown paper against her palms.

But she understood now, as she did then, the expectation that filled the faces of those around her, remembered, too, the exhilarating feeling of body and mind moving forward together in a world that made sense. So she took the pills that Chloe lined up in brightly colored boxes on the kitchen table, even as she knew that they were not a solution, that they only held her artificially aloft and that one day she would plummet, Icarus-like, into an unnavigable sea below.

She had made a resolution to stop it all before she hit the water and was gone—the pills Chloe gave her were not the only ones she had access to. The problem was, there were no notes left behind from those who had gone before her, no helpful explanations to tell her when the break point would be, that last exquisite moment of engagement with the world before you fell, leaving only a body for others to care for. If, in fact, there was a moment, a definitive before-and-after point. She was coming to believe more and more these days that her mind was like a boyfriend who would show up with flowers just when you had decided you were ready to dump him, the hope of the bouquets overriding the knowledge that they were getting smaller and smaller each time.

But even if there was a moment of recognition, would she be able to do it—make the decision, leap before she fell? She hadn't left her husband, after all. She had stayed, even as she felt herself disappearing—she always said it was for the children, but by the time Edward actually left, they were all well into college. She had never taken a voluntary exit, but once the door was opened for her and she stepped out, she found she was greedy for every minute of her own life. Which, of course, made the prospect of willingly turning her back on it now, when she might have even one more moment left, all the more difficult.

Isabelle looked down at the people around her. Interesting, she thought, what a difference a few feet made; she could see them all so much more clearly from up here. Her Rory had gone quiet, Abby's body practically sending off sparks in his direction; Tom and Lillian hid on opposite sides of the throne, looking at anything but each other. Chloe was walking next to Al, laughing at some joke he had told, actively ignoring Finnegan. They were like ingredients that had become chemically incapable of mixing with each other, or perhaps had simply forgotten how, when she knew it wasn't the case and didn't need to be. Didn't they realize that a day like today, this ritual that Al had found, was more about all of them than it could ever be about her?

She wanted to tell them, but as she started to speak, she spotted a woman she thought she should recognize, standing on the sidewalk, staring at Chloe and Al with such hostility that Isabelle had to look away. When she looked back, the woman was gone.

Who was she? Isabelle wondered. She knew she should know, but it was the anger she recognized more than the woman, and it sideswiped her into memories. Edward introducing his secretary like a prize he'd won at the county fair. Edward coming home from work and propping himself against the kitchen doorway, his eyes taking in the scene in front of him as if he was the manager of a corporation with one employee, her, and a raise was not forthcoming. She would feel his scrutiny and think of her day, the children roiling around her like a sea of eels, the housework piling up into towers, the way she had managed to settle the water, turn it all into a sweet domestic scene before his arrival so he would find a calm and lovely wife wearing makeup and a neat, trim dress in the kitchen preparing his meal.

She hadn't even known how much she'd hated it until he was gone. The day the divorce was finalized, she had wandered through the uninhabited rooms of their home and realized that every memory of her children was still being filtered through Edward's eyes. It wasn't until the house was sold and she was on the road that she could feel her love for her children, her life, flowing through her like a clean, cool river.

She looked down at Rory and Abby, each holding up one of the front rails. Her children.

It was going to be hardest on Abby, what was coming. For all that Abby had yearned to be a grown-up when she was a child, the aspects of adulthood that she seemed to treasure most, ironically, were the ones that held her to the ground instead of letting her go. Abby was truly comfortable only when she could contain and shape a memory, a plan in her own hands. She held on so tightly to an idea of family that she often overlooked the people within her own.

More than once, Isabelle had envisioned herself as a balloon in Abby's life, helping to lift her daughter off the ground she clung to so desperately, although Isabelle doubted her daughter saw the value in this. But now Isabelle wondered, as she sat on the jostling chair—what would happen if there were no balloon pulling her daughter upward? Perhaps gravity might seem less attractive if it wasn't helping you hold something else to the earth. Perhaps you could simply, finally, let go.

The streamers on Isabelle's throne fluttered in the early spring breeze, trailing out behind. Isabelle could feel the air moving across her face, the voices of the people below her. She closed her eyes and let her mind relax. She was up in the sky, the engine of the crop duster vibrating beneath her feet as it soared over the fields and the spectators in the bandstands. Isabelle stood, feeling the motion below, and opened her arms to the world around her.

The

WALKABOUT

Christ, Abby sighed, looking at the glacial impasse of her mother's closet, she'd never get her moved out of here.

She'd heard stories from her friends—they were all facing the same thing—about the endless negotiations, a mother's refusal to give up a silver chafing dish or jars of coriander or cayenne pepper so old and dusty that their contents could have been interchanged without any impact on flavor. Attics and garages packed with bassinets and badminton rackets, hand-painted bird feeders, six-packs of Bud Light for a husband who had died ten years before—boxes of now grown children's artwork pushing up through it all like underbrush among trees.

"Every forest needs a fire occasionally to be healthy,"

Abby's friend Janey had said to her own mother, only to be proudly shown a collection of Smokey the Bear paintings Janey had created when she was seven.

It had become a favorite topic of conversation among Abby's female friends at parties. And it was the women, Abby thought. While the men were discussing sports and gadgets, the women talked about their children, their parents—the way as soon as one set grew up, the other started falling apart, just when you had finally spotted a clean and unencumbered horizon.

"Every damn safety pin has a thirty-minute story attached," Janey had complained to Abby after a weekend at her parents' home. "It's like trying to move a freaking elephant."

Abby nodded. She'd seen it with Isabelle, the way things could become so permeated with memories that story was more important than function. She'd watched her brother listening to Isabelle's meandering tales of the china that had been used once, on a great-grandmother's wedding day, before her husband ran off with her sister. The way, after the story had made its journey from the china to Rory's ears, the plates themselves seemed to take up less space, become almost expendable.

If she could just get some interesting stories, Abby thought, it might be bearable. But Abby would pick the seemingly most innocuous item in a drawer—a rusty garlic press, a third bottle opener—thinking it might be a good icebreaker, the easy thing to pitch into the trash or charity pile and give her mother the rush of weightlessness that came from getting rid of things, a feeling that just might steamroll them through a whole shelf, a drawer—only to be sucked into an endless explanation of how that particular opener was necessary to open the special bottles of soda Rory liked to drink in the summer. And Abby would close her mouth against the desire to tell her mother that they didn't even make that kind of soda anymore and that Rory, when he visited, if he visited, always came in the fall or spring.

Where had all this stuff come from? Abby wondered, looking at her mother's closet. Isabelle had taken almost nothing to that cabin when she'd sold their family home. She'd moved into the city only ten years ago. And yet, she had managed to accumulate quite a pile. The prospect of the sheer weight of her mother's belongings landing on Abby's head, in her garage, made her feel slightly desperate. Abby couldn't imagine what would happen to the few islands of order and sanity that existed in her life if she was forced to admit entry to the hoards of her mother's possessions.

It was easier when the question of keep-or-pitch could be laid at the door of less personal offenders—mold, dust, insects—agents of destruction Abby had always viewed with abhorrence, now her main allies in the winnowing of her mother's belongings.

"You can't keep this," she would tell her mother, holding up a sweater Swiss-cheesed by moths.

"Don't you like the color?" Isabelle would answer.

Sometimes, at the end of a particularly unproductive sorting session, Abby would find herself sneaking objects into her purse, to be disposed of later with a relief that seemed far more satisfying than she was comfortable with.

Although, of course, Isabelle always noticed. Abby wondered how her mother, who couldn't even remember her own grandchild's name, could always seem to spot when something was missing.

"I had it on my desk," she would tell Abby over the phone. Not "How was your flight home?" Not "Thank you for coming." Just "Do you know where my black stapler is?"

And yet, Abby thought, looking in her mother's closet, in all those thousands of objects, there was not one sign of Abby's father, as if, when he left, the vacuum he created sucked all evidence of him from her mother's life.

WHEN ABBY WAS GROWING UP, her father was the briefcase by the front door, the man reading the paper on Sundays. He was not at her dance recitals or the science fair. He was not behind the wheel, picking her up after a high school dance. She didn't expect him to be, any more than her friends expected their fathers to fly. Abby had learned early on the tricks to pull the high beams of her father's attention in her direction. He liked things straight and clean; he believed in hard work and charts with stars, and Abby conscientiously filled in the one she had put on the refrigerator door, even when her mother laughed and said love wasn't born in boxes.

That was just the kind of thing Abby's mother was always saying. As if she had any idea of how the world worked. She, who had once driven the kids to school in her bathrobe when the alarm didn't go off and Abby had woken them all up in a panic. Even when she was young, Abby understood why her father sometimes treated her mother as if she was one of the children. Given the choice, Abby would have followed her father to work. She had visited his office when she was five and had fallen in love with its white walls and clean surfaces. People had commented on her intelligence, calling her the little doctor. She had wanted to stay there forever.

Lucy and Rory, snuggled together beneath the overhang of Abby's status as eldest, never saw things the way she did. They viewed their mother as imaginative, creative, fun—the only mom on the block who would play with the kids. They didn't see the way their mother's paint-splattered blouses were viewed by the neighbors, or catch the disappointment in their father's eyes. Abby's siblings had been well asleep on the nights when Abby snuck downstairs to eavesdrop on their parents at the dinner table—the tense cutting and chewing of food and words. Lucy and Rory had never sat on the staircase, bent legs stiffening into wishbones, willing the two people at the table to be a family, knowing she could make it work if only she sat there long enough.

And it had worked, for years—although neither her parents nor her siblings seemed particularly grateful for her efforts. Rory had been sanguine about their parents' breakup when it happened; he said that their mother deserved to be her own person, finally. Rory, the budding archaeologist, studying to become the collector of everyone's past, had had no trouble letting go of his own. And Lucy, twenty years old at that point, enthralled with her new baby and a proselyte to a vision of a liberated motherhood, could only look at her mother's marriage with a kind of hormone-drenched sympathy.

Lucy still wasn't much more help, when it came right down to it. Lucy had moved to Australia more than twenty-five years ago—permanent walkabout, Abby's husband, Bob, liked to call it—and had come home just a few times since. Abby and Bob had visited her once, before Rory was born. Lucy's brood had swarmed down the steps of a big old farmhouse to meet them, and Abby and Bob had spent the week in a world of tie-dye and chicken coops. Abby watched her sister, unable to decide if she was completely frustrated by Lucy's *It will all work out* attitude or jealous because it always seemed to.

These days, Abby would call her sister over those gazillion miles of phone cable and try and make plans for their mother, and Lucy would merely laugh and tell Abby to chill out. Lucy seemed to view their mother's illness through a gauzy sentimentality, Alzheimer's benevolently offering their mother a kind of fugue state where Isabelle would be blessed with the experience of relating simply to her own senses and emotions.

"Wouldn't it be nice not to worry sometimes, Abby?" Lucy had asked.

Except that particular fairy tale held up only if you were thousands of miles away, geographically relieved of responsibility. If you lived nearby, a plane hop, if you did any research at all, you could see what was coming. The slow disintegration of personality, inhibitions giving way to frustration and anger and paranoia. The increasing inability to read and write and eventually eat or speak. It wasn't easy, or sweet, or lovely. The studies said that thirty percent of caregivers died before their patients. Cold, hard facts—which you didn't have to be a doctor to find out about.

When Abby was younger, her mother had, for several years, driven all three children up the coast to the cabin that Isabelle had inherited the spring Abby turned seven. The drive was long, the children restless, and in an effort to keep their minds and bodies contained, their mother had told them stories. Back then, Isabelle's stories had been capacious, three-dimensional affairs, illuminated by particulars—the quality of light on a wall in France, the iridescence of a woman's midnight-blue cocktail dress—

the imagery sneaking into the book Abby was trying to read, while Lucy and Rory sat listening, mouths open in fascination.

And every year, they had passed an ancient barn on the side of the highway about two-thirds of the way through the trip, when the long, blond stretches of California gave way to the trees and saturated greens of Oregon. Abby noticed the barn the first time, its gray boards sagging under the weight of years and weather, and each year after it became a competition to see who could spot it first.

Rory and Lucy were fascinated by the barn and the tales their mother would make up about its history and the land around it, the generations of people who had lived there. Each year, the rafters of the barn seemed to be swooning a bit deeper, as if bowing toward a gentler time. But Abby's siblings never seemed to see the inexorability of it all, the reality of boards finally splayed flat on the ground; they focused on the barn, when the real power lay in gravity. They still hadn't learned that lesson.

"Be with her now," Rory had said as he and Abby argued in the bedroom of their mother's house that afternoon.

But who was going to be with her later? Abby wondered, staring at her mother's closet. Chloe was an almost acceptable stopgap measure, but Isabelle was getting to a point where she needed more structured care and it would be up to Abby, the doctor daughter living in San

Francisco—which was at least on the same coast, the same continent, for God's sake—to be the bad guy in the situation. *That* role she could remember.

"See anything you like?" Isabelle came up next to Abby and peered into the closet.

"It's a bit full," Abby remarked.

"Indeed." Isabelle nodded thoughtfully. "We'll need to do something about that someday."

"RORY, seriously, we have to have a plan."

Abby had cornered her brother in the kitchen. They had done the neighborhood processional, carrying about that bizarre chair, enduring the stares of the neighbors. They'd avoided catastrophe. (Thank God for that tall boy catching Isabelle when she stood. What the hell had she been thinking, anyway?) Now they were home and her mother was safe on the living room couch, flanked by the woman chef and Chloe.

"I don't want to have this conversation today," Rory said to Abby.

"Which just means I'll do it."

"Abby," he said, shaking his head in frustration, "do you ever stop to think that if you didn't do it, we might?"

Memories swarmed in Abby's head. Rory about to head off to the high school prom having completely forgotten the corsage for his date, Abby stealing a rose from the next-door neighbor's yard and making one with the pink ribbon she'd saved from a birthday present. Lucy, sixteen, pregnant; Abby finding the abortion clinic. Not telling Mom. Abby, going to their father ten years ago, making sure that Isabelle was covered in his will, regardless of the second wife, the second family.

"No," Abby said to her brother. "I don't."

ABBY WENT OUT into the backyard and pulled out her cell phone, exhaling in relief when she heard her husband pick up the line.

"Bob?" she said. "Talk me down."

"Is it your mom or your siblings?"

"Both."

"Well, then. Come home." His voice warm, seductively matter-of-fact.

"I swear to God it's like they're all channeling Deepak Chopra. I'm going to kill someone."

"You won't."

"I just needed to hear your voice."

"I know. I love you. Fly safe."

She could tell from his almost imperceptible restraint that she was skittering in and out of the "Isabelle's daughter voice" that drove him crazy, but he was too kind, or smart, to say anything about it just then. It always took her a couple of days to get back to herself after a trip to her mother's—family lag, she and Bob called it—but they were used to the transitions by now. Abby recalled, with the first real smile of her day, how, about day three, he would come home from the office, look at her and say, "There you are," and take her off to bed.

"I love you, too," she said, reaching inside for the Abby he knew, and almost, but not quite, finding her. "See you soon."

She ended the call and sat down on the back steps, looking at her mother's throne.

ABBY COULD STILL REMEMBER meeting Bob in college, the absolute luxury of finding someone who saw the world as she did, who took care of her in the way she took care of everything else. Bob was her match, her equal—something she could not have said for the boys she had known in high school, who always needed to borrow her class notes, or help them get over the girl before her. And Bob didn't care that she was his equal—a rarity, really, even in the 1970s, when everyone was supposed to be liberated.

Abby's brother, Rory, had commented early on that Bob was like their father. In private, Abby was willing to concede that there were some similarities in drive and ability. Abby was not her mother, however, and therein lay the difference.

"But is he any fun?" Lucy had asked. "I mean, how's the sex?"

A discussion Abby did not enter into with her younger

sister, who had seemed to view sex as a grown-up version of finger-painting, sensual and delightfully messy, and perhaps—although Abby only suspected this—best done as a group activity. Abby, on the other hand, who had taken enough biology classes to know the failure rate of every contraceptive on the market, had never considered the idea of sex with anyone who was not strong potential father material. And thus Bob was the first, something she did not disclose to her sister, but the reality was that sex with an equal was something startling and exciting in a way that Lucy had certainly never described. Bob met Abby's eyes and held them.

They had waited until Abby's medical practice was established to have a baby, and even afterward had made sure to keep the romance of their relationship alive. Date night, every week—and not some talk-about-our-child kind of dinner, like so many of their friends. Abby and Bob made an occasion of their evenings together. They got a regular babysitter for Rory early on, a matronly woman in her sixties, expensive, but it was worth it to have evenings that didn't start with a screaming baby. They found restaurants that served unusual dishes, dressed for dinner, kept up on the news, stayed interesting for each other.

And at the end of the evening, they would go home to bed, and Bob would look in her eyes and the connection was so powerful in its clarity that she knew, without a doubt, that she was loved. When her friends told her of their husbands admitting to affairs, of their shock and surprise, she could only surmise they must have sex with their eyes closed. If Bob ever cheated on her, Abby would need only one look to know.

No, Abby thought, she was not her mother's daughter. Nor her father's.

ABBY WALKED BACK in the house and saw her mother talking on the phone in her bedroom, smiling. Then Isabelle laid the receiver on the nightstand and wandered off down the hallway. Abby went over and picked up the phone with a sigh.

"Rory?" Abby heard her sister on the phone, the crackle of static. "Hey little brother, that was quick. How're you doing? Is Captain Abby driving you crazy?" Lucy laughed.

"Yes," Abby said. "I believe she is."

"Oh, geez, Abs. I'm sorry." The laugh again.

"How are you, Lucy?" Abby asked.

"Terrific." Lucy changed the subject effortlessly. "The kids are great. The grandkids are great. I wish I could just put Mom on a plane and get her here so she could meet them all."

When Abby was taking psychology classes in college, she had often thought of personalities as things children tried on in utero, choosing traits that fit them out of the closet of parental options. Lucy seemed to have taken only from their mother. Full of imagination, unconcerned about what the neighbors thought—in many ways, she would be the better caretaker. The house would still be full of junk ten years after their mother died, of course, but everybody would be oh so happy.

Why couldn't I be like that? Abby wondered; but that wasn't how it worked. Somebody had to be serious. Families were like puzzles; in the end, there were only so many shapes, and so many places to put them in. Otherwise you just had a bunch of pieces.

"That would be nice, Lucy."

"Abby, honey, you need to relax. Are you doing that yoga tape I sent you?"

Abby did Pilates three times a week. She had donated Lucy's tape to the library, slipping it through the drop slot with a mixed feeling of contrition and virtuousness that it was, after all, not the trash can.

"Sure," Abby said.

"You're breathing from your diaphragm?"

"Of course."

"And you're visualizing a healthy mind for Mom?"

Okay, that was enough.

Abby closed the bedroom door. "Lucy, you do *not* get to sit out there on your never-ending walkabout and ask me if I'm visualizing a healthy mind for Mom."

"Maybe you should try it."

"I'm a doctor. I don't visualize; I heal."

"No, I mean a walkabout."

"Lucy, I've got people to take care of here. Our mother, for one."

"Abby—" And now Lucy sounded her age, and sad. "There's a difference between taking care of and caring for. That's something I learned on my silly little walkabout, actually. Think about it."

"RORY." Abby walked up to her son, who was sitting with Isabelle on the couch. "Time to go."

"Seriously?" Rory checked his watch. "I mean, the plane's not for three hours yet."

"Traffic," said Abby. "And we have to return the rental car."

"Okay." Rory shrugged. Abby thought she caught him rolling his eyes as he reached over and kissed his grandmother on the cheek, but it was probably just the light. She'd been meaning to get her vision checked for distance glasses. The ability to read expressions was important when you were a doctor, the way a parent's face could tell you more about a child's condition than any thermometer or blood test ever would.

Isabelle started to get to her feet.

"Don't get up, Mom," Abby said, bending down. "I'm sorry," she said, as she hugged her mother. "I have to go."

"I know," Isabelle replied.

"Ready to go, Mom?" Rory came up next to Abby, his backpack slung over his shoulder.

. . .

SITTING IN THE RENTAL CAR in her mother's driveway, Abby took a deep breath. The day was over. She'd made it. The jubilation of being out of the house pulsed through her—followed by immediate, horrified shame at her relief, and the unsettling realization that she'd done it again.

Every time, it was like this—as if the very act of entering her mother's house was a Pavlovian stimulus that caused her to shed all her best years in a rapid-fire return to aggravated adolescence. It was only after she left that she could pick those good years back up and put them on, grateful for the warmth of some, the spine-strengthening experience of others. The grown-up Abby would shake her head and swear it wouldn't happen next time, knowing of course it would.

But it was too late to do anything about it this time, she told herself, and with one turn of the key in the ignition, she would be on her way home, where there would be whole beans waiting to be ground into coffee in the morning, San Francisco out her window, and appointments ticking off like dominoes falling through the day. Even though the children she saw in her pediatric practice were hardly orderly, their emotional baggage was still of the carry-on variety, their needs simple—a brightly colored Band-Aid after the prick of a needle, a splash of affection to hurry along the effects of an antibiotic or a pain reliever.

And her own son, while he wasn't always perfect (look at all that sugar he had given his grandmother; did Abby really have to wait until his prefrontal cortex kicked in at twenty-five before she could expect reasonable adult behavior from him?), he was hers, the road map of their interactions well traveled, the route chosen long ago.

Key in hand, she could feel herself yearning toward the bright and seductive busyness that was her normal life. Going to her mother's house always felt like shifting into second gear while she was still traveling at sixty-five miles an hour. Abby had watched Lillian and Isabelle washing the dishes this afternoon, drifting about the kitchen like lazy underwater creatures, and it was all she could do not to grab the plates right out of their hands. If only they had let her, she could have had it all done in five minutes. Without breakage.

She couldn't wait to be home, to let loose the unused energy that had been building all day. She smiled at the thought of all she would get done when she let it free. She could feel her chin rising, her mouth relaxing, grown-up Abby returning to the world. She could almost look in the rearview mirror without worrying that a teenager would be staring back at her.

Which was a good thing, because her own adolescent was fidgeting in the seat next to her.

"Mom?" Rory said. "Did you forget something?"

Abby looked at her son, checking for irony in his words, detecting only an edge of frustration. She shouldn't have dragged him up here; it must be awful to be around a grandmother who didn't even recognize him. She should have put his needs first; she should have said he couldn't come when Chloe called, all excited about that ridiculous ritual. Abby was already planning her mother's eightieth, anyway. She had a guest list almost fifty people long, and she could make it longer—she might even get Lucy to bring her brood. She'd heard the Westin hotel did an excellent salmon dinner.

Rory sighed. He was tired, Abby thought; they both were. It had been a long day. Abby remembered those months when her son was learning to walk, her hands perpetually outstretched to catch him if he fell, adrenaline shooting into her veins at the slightest sway of his toddler legs. She had forgotten what that felt like until today, watching her mother teeter her way through the world, every step, every carpet edge a trip hazard, every teapot a potential scalding incident.

"Mom," Rory said, "can we go now?"

Abby started the car and backed out of her mother's driveway, heading for the airport, the first step of the trip back to her own family.

ABBY DROVE THE CAR down the darkened street, past the lights in the neighboring houses. From her pediatric practice, Abby knew that people could be remarkably different than what they seemed when viewed from the outside—the professional mother who couldn't manage to remember to change a Band-Aid, which led to infection; the out-of-work dad, bringing his kids in for their annual appointments, the unstated and slightly guilty joy he got out of his proximity to their small lives. You just didn't know what was going on in people's houses. Or heads, Abby thought.

Her siblings, her mother, thought they knew her. But they didn't know. They didn't know her marriage, they didn't know who she was. They saw no-nonsense, no-sex Abby. Captain Abby, the Portable Planner. They saw what they needed to see, the big sister, the daughter who made their lives work, in concert or contrast. With her as a hub of the family wheel, Rory could run around the world, Lucy could be the sexy earth mother, Isabelle could hold on to that goddamn cabin until she died, always knowing that Abby would be answering the phone, loyal, capable, and deeply uninteresting.

Abby flicked on the turn indicator and headed right.

Well, she hadn't always been good. And she'd been tempted. Anybody who said they hadn't was either lying or had the sex life that Abby's siblings always assumed she did. But Abby had known better than to risk losing Bob for one of the adrenaline-fueled relationships of medical school or, later, the charmingly panicked eyes of a new father bringing his child to her office.

There was one time, though, a guy in college, a near

miss as it were. She'd never told Bob and certainly not Lucy or Rory. Abby hadn't been going out with Bob long at that point—she had met him at the end of their freshman year, just a couple of weeks before summer vacation began, and then they had gone home to opposite sides of the country. Abby had spent the summer in Los Angeles with her parents and younger siblings, in a household that seemed ready to crack at the seams.

She had gotten a job at her father's office, answering phones. Work was clean, white, and simple. The phones rang; she answered them. Her father's secretary was helpful, treating her more like a daughter than an employee, taking her out to lunch that first day, giving her tips on dressing professionally, listening to Abby's plans for medical school.

It wasn't glamorous, but it was money for tuition and it got her out of the house, where her mother seemed to be whirling in increasingly smaller circles. Abby had read a short story in her mandatory college literature class about a crazy woman who crawled around a room, rubbing away the wallpaper with her shoulder. In the evenings that summer, when she got home from work, Abby would check the wallpaper in the dining room, but all she ever found were the marks she and her siblings had made where they leaned back in their chairs as children. Yet when Abby tried to have normal conversations with her mother, tell her stories about the real world, about how well Abby was doing and how helpful her father's secretary was, her mother just turned her back and ignored her, saying she had to make dinner.

It was so much better to be somewhere else, even if it was in her head. She and Bob spent the months of that summer apart, writing each other, their letters becoming increasingly passionate and explicit. She could almost feel his breath coming off the pages of his letters, sliding across her neck, up behind her ears. When an envelope appeared in the mailbox, she took it to her room and locked the door, her hands straying as she read the words, over and over. She wrote back, fantasies of dresses with too many buttons, the slide of a hand down the curve of a back. At night, when everyone else was asleep, she went outside and stood by the pool. The neighborhood was silent, all the windows dark. Above her, a few stars managed to burst their way into the sky above Los Angeles. Abby imagined taking off her clothes, lowering herself into the pool and pushing off the edge, the water, still warm from the afternoon sun, slipping over her as she swam.

ON HER LAST DAY OF WORK, Abby went by her father's office to see if he wanted to go to lunch. Really, he should have asked her.

"Edward," Brenda, her father's secretary, was always

saying, "girls don't stay this age forever. You should take her out to lunch while you can."

But that day, Abby decided she would take the initiative. She was going back to school in a week; she'd probably never see him during that time if she wasn't at the office.

She walked toward his office and looked in the partially opened door. Brenda was leaning over the desk, handing him a stack of papers. Her father was looking up at her, and the expression on his face was something Abby had seen only in the movies.

ABBY HAD RETURNED HOME to an empty house, mind and body shaking. Lucy and Rory were off at a summer job or the beach, depending. On the kitchen counter, she found a note from her mother, saying she was off grocery shopping and would be back soon.

Couldn't her mother do anything more exciting? And Abby knew all the boring things that would be in the bags her mother brought home. Abby had discovered alfalfa sprouts that spring, and sandwiches with avocado and real cheddar cheese. Her mother, on the other hand, seemed to have awoken in the 1950s, like a culinary Sleeping Beauty, and decided that was where she was going to stay. Compared with the womanly elegance, the sophisticated palate of her father's secretary, Isabelle was about as exciting as a grilled Velveeta sandwich, a dish they'd had more than once for dinner.

Her mother probably didn't even know about Brenda, Abby thought as she went upstairs.

At the top, where she should have turned right to go down the hall to her bedroom, Abby turned left. She used to go that way when she was young and nightmares ripped her out of sleep. She had stopped when her father told her that big sisters made it through the night in their own beds. But now she went into her parents' bedroom, opening the closet, gazing at their clothes as if the arrangement would give her an understanding of what was happening. Her mother's shoes were lined up in a row leading directly to her father's, the dresses hanging neatly right next to the suits. It was almost possible to believe that the crackling sound of her parents' marriage that summer, the expression on her father's face that afternoon, was only the heat of August—except everybody knew that heat didn't do that in Los Angeles.

Abby walked over to the bed, touching the surface of the spread, the pillows plumped into mounds. She ran her fingers over the round brass clock on her mother's nightstand, and then opened the drawer below. Inside were earplugs, a pencil and an unmarked pad of paper, and in the back, a small, blue oval machine with a round attachment at one end, a white electrical cord at the other. Abby didn't immediately recognize it, and then, suddenly, she did. Her college roommate, Sandra, had one; she had shown Abby, joking about fish and bicycles and not needing men.

Abby shut the drawer of her mother's nightstand with a quick, definitive click and went down the hall to her own room.

ABBY AND BOB had returned to college in the fall, almost embarrassed when they saw each other. The reality of Bob, of Abby, rattled loosely inside the fantasies they had created of one another over the summer, and it was disconcerting to be touched by hands instead of words. It was easier and more familiar when they were at a distance, even across a room, the space between them filled with the things they had said on paper, the air shivering with possibility. Which was how it still was that first day of the term, when the guy came into the chemistry lab, took one look at Abby, and chose her as his partner.

His hair was red and curly, not her type at all. He was a music major, just taking chemistry for fun, he said. Nothing like Bob, who was a choice Abby had made the first moment she saw him. And yet, when the red-haired guy reached for the beaker and his hand came near hers, she held still, hoping his hand would continue on its trajectory, brush her skin and tangle its way into her hair. Back in her dorm room that night, she found herself imagining a deserted lab, a metal table swept clean of all equipment, its hard surface cool against the length of her back as he rose above her.

She knew he wasn't the one she wanted, but her body wouldn't stop rustling, and a few mornings later, when she went to get dressed and realized she didn't have any clean underwear, she paused, hand raised over the laundry basket, midway to grabbing a pair from the day before. Then she pulled her hand back. She walked to the closet and selected a skirt, the fabric sliding over her bare skin like a suggestion.

It was amazing, she thought, as she walked across the campus, how the absence of something could be more startling than its presence had ever been. Each step seemed to have a bigger, more directed purpose, the rustling in her body concentrating, becoming almost, delectably, unbearable. She was suddenly aware of the pink-tipped flowers of the floss-silk trees that lined the walkway, the smell of bacon and eggs coming from the cafeteria, the air moving between her legs like the lightest of fingertips. Abby wondered if the guy in the chemistry lab would know, what he would do if he did.

"Hey."

She heard Bob's voice behind her, felt his hand on her shoulder. "Missing breakfast this morning?"

She turned and his eyes caught hers, looked again.

"Walk you to class?" he asked.

She nodded, and they fell in line next to each other, his arm firm around her waist. She could see the straight lines of the classroom buildings at the end of the walkway in front of them. Her body softened against his, the long line of his leg moving against hers, and his hand slipped slowly lower, finally reaching what wasn't there. She heard an intake of breath, felt his pace catch and right itself, and then Bob's arm changed their course, back to her dormitory.

"YOU'RE GOING THE WRONG WAY, Mom," Rory said.

"What?" She couldn't even remember driving the last few blocks. Her eyes took in the black matte surface of the rental car dashboard, the glowing lights of speedometer, odometer.

"This isn't the way to the airport," Rory said.

"Yes, it is."

"Mom, you're going to the grocery store."

Abby understood condescension to be a natural byproduct of adolescence, arriving along with sweat and armpit hair. She observed it in her patients all the time, although when boys reached that age they generally moved on to male doctors, whose voices were lower and whose body parts, although never seen, were assumed to be similar. You couldn't take the defection personally.

"I don't think so." Her doctor's voice, as her mother would say.

"Then what's that?" Rory pointed to the neon sign that read FOOD MART.

"Oh hell," Abby said. Of course it was. How many times had she taken her mother to this very store in the past ten years? Isabelle drifting along, pushing the cart, Abby offering to run ahead and return with the items on her mother's list. Who wouldn't want their own personal shopper, anyway? But Isabelle would just say she wanted to choose her own tomatoes.

"Damn it." Abby abruptly swerved into the left lane and entered the intersection at full speed, cranking the steering wheel into a U-turn.

"Mom!" Rory exclaimed. "Red light!"

And then, louder, panicked, "CAR!"

Abby heard the scream of brakes, looked to her right and saw headlights coming at her son, illuminating his profile, so much like her brother's. The hair that wouldn't quite lie flat, the cheekbones and chin that were becoming stronger as he grew into himself. Rory, her boy. The boy running across the soccer field, or sprawled on the couch with them, watching a movie. Without thinking, she flung her right arm across him and punched the accelerator through the rest of her turn, vaulting her car out of the intersection. In the rearview mirror, she saw a car fly behind her, just missing her rear bumper. An old blue Cadillac, fins rising up in the back. A blond woman in the driver's seat, flipping her off.

Abby pulled over to the curb, breathing hard.

"Mom, Jesus Christ," Rory said.

"Are you okay?" She touched his arm, his hair. Nothing missing.

"Mom?" he asked. "Should I be driving?"

She stopped, her hand in the air.

She recognized that tone; it had come out of her mouth as recently as this afternoon. The readiness, the desire, to take over, a modulation set midway between frustration and condescension. As if Isabelle was a child, or worse, so far gone that childhood would be an improvement. It had seemed justified at the time, a minor venting of a larger aggravation. She hadn't even really thought about how it might appear to her mother.

Now she had a pretty good idea. When had her own child become her? Abby wondered.

The timing was ironic, in so many ways. Abby could still remember her own teenage certainty that she was smarter, more capable than her mother. She had never stopped believing it, if she was honest. And yet only today, as she had listened to her mother's conversation circle and repeat, observed the blankness in Isabelle's eyes when she had first seen her grandson, Abby understood for the first time the difference between adolescent hubris and actual responsibility and wanted nothing more than to give the latter back. In that moment, she had realized that perhaps all she'd ever wanted, all any child wanted, was to feel the exhilarating wind of independence rushing about her, flying without needing to land.

But there wasn't any choice, really. Gravity would always win, Abby knew that much. Isabelle would continue down the path she was on, and sooner or later Abby would follow her. Her own son would see himself as smarter than she, and then perhaps that would change, and change again. If they both were lucky, her son would never experience the difference between certainty and understanding when it came to his mother. But in the end, there was nothing she could do to alter any of it. They were all just barns, swooning toward the earth; the only thing that held them up was stories.

The smell of burning brakes still hung in the air. Abby looked over at her son, alive in the passenger seat next to her.

She took a deep breath and turned the key in the ignition.

"Where are you going, Mom?" Rory asked cautiously.

"Back," she said. "I forgot something."

Abby put the car in gear and headed to Isabelle's house.

The

WOODPILE

Tom was furious, or perhaps merely frightened. He had realized over the past five years how similar the two emotions could appear, dressing up in each other's clothes like friends who had spent far too much time together. But the sight of Isabelle's handprint across Lillian's stomach—everything he suddenly realized it meant, and the fact that she hadn't told him—left his brain with such a cacophony of feelings that he had fled the kitchen. He had managed to avoid Lillian during Isabelle's parade through the neighborhood, always seeing a streamer that required refastening or a need for assistance on the other side of Isabelle's throne. When the afternoon was over and good-byes were drifting across the evening air, he ducked out to Isabelle's garden. Maybe there he would be able to line up his emotions in neat rows, weed out the ones that didn't belong.

Isabelle's chair rested at the edge of the vegetable patch. He wasn't sure if it was proper for him to sit in someone else's throne, but the chair didn't seem to mind, its deep expanse an undeniable invitation. He raised himself onto its seat and the arms enclosed him. He let out his breath for what felt like the first time in hours and shut his eyes.

Suddenly, he heard the screaming of car brakes, no more than a few blocks away. His body seized, waiting for the inevitable collision, the sound of metal scraping through the crackling surface of glass. But it didn't happen. He heard only the swerve, a shifting of speed and direction, realignment. The neighborhood quieted again.

That was how it was supposed to work, he thought—a momentary jostling with mortality that awoke you to life's possibilities, the fact that you had been wasting your days being frustrated about that extra-long red light on your way to work or the fact that the grocery store no longer stocked your favorite brand of cereal. You would look up, startled, and then go forward into the world, thankful for the reprieve.

Except, of course, when it didn't happen that way—when fate just kept coming and took out not you but someone so close to you that you wished its aim had been better. And once it happened, it was like you were snagged in that moment, always waiting, always ready to fall.

That was the thing he didn't know how to explain to anybody, even himself—the way that grief was a country as difficult to leave as it had been terrible to enter. Right now he should be rejoicing at the prospect of life in this new woman he loved. And yet all it took was one blast of adrenaline and he was flailing his way back down the rabbit hole of Charlie's death.

IT SHOULD HAVE BEEN A SIGN, a billboard, that nothing was ever going to make sense again—the surreal way the first days after Charlie's diagnosis had reminded him of arriving in Italy on their honeymoon. One moment he had been on an American plane, a practicing lawyer, newly married, listening to announcements in a language that entered his consciousness effortlessly, seamlessly. The next, he was in an airport where nothing—the signs, the conversations, the gestures—was comprehensible.

It was only a few years later that he sat next to his wife in a doctor's office, hearing a diagnosis that was no more intelligible.

Over time, he had learned to navigate the country of illness. The multisyllabic vocabulary that sounded like Greek and sometimes was. The customs—when to offer help, when to pull back, when a compliment would be considered anything other than pity, when a hand on an elbow would provide more support than pain. And the traditions—the glass of wine Charlie was never supposed to drink, a moment to remember who they had been when the only language they didn't know was Italian.

"Here's to the day," she would say, raising her glass, while he tried not to remember the nights of their honeymoon, her breasts round and full as she walked toward him across their hotel room.

But it seemed no sooner had he become fluent in caretaking than he was exiled to the country of widowers, where he lived in a house stuffed with silence. He spent months unable to speak to others, no longer knowing how and uninterested in learning. People sent notes on stiff, white stationery, consoled him on his loss—and it was all he could do not to scream at them that he hadn't *lost* anything; he had never let her out of his sight; there was no losing here. There was only leaving.

His friends worried as time passed and he evinced no signs of moving forward, but when they reminded him that he was young and encouraged him to look outward and move on, the thought of conversing, of having to learn the vocabulary and nuances of another lover's (he couldn't think wife's) needs and life story, was exhausting. It was easier to speak a language he knew, even if he was talking to a dead woman.

It was almost a year after Charlie's death that a friend took him to Lillian's restaurant and Tom found an announcement for cooking classes on the table. He had signed up, surprising himself. Perhaps it had felt like a way to still be with Charlie, who had loved food so completely that he sometimes joked there was no room left for him—a claim Charlie had defiantly and abundantly refuted, her arms and legs wrapped around him, her long blond hair smelling of olive oil and oregano and simmering tomatoes, scents he should be jealous of but could only inhale, completely and utterly seduced.

But in the end, Lillian's cooking class had become a beginning of sorts. Somewhere around the third class he had felt his senses start to awaken, had found himself savoring the crunch of toast in the morning, the warm glide of butter across his tongue. He had looked around him at the other people in the class, wondering about their stories, their sadnesses and joys.

And then one evening, in class, he had stood next to Lillian at the counter and watched her long, slim fingers moving through flour, gripping the handle of a pan. From hands, it was a slow but simple progression to wrists, arms, collarbones, eyes. The way her lips would relax into a small, satisfied smile as the shreds of cheese in a fondue finally melded together. The way she would watch her students, the sense he got that she was giving them what they needed, even as she withheld something from herself. The latter intrigued him most, perhaps, and he began to observe her more closely, looking for the thing that she was missing, hoping it might have something to do with him.

The similarities between Charlie and Lillian were obvious—their mutual love of food, the way they changed others' lives through the simple act of feeding them. But where Charlie had been the warmth of sun on a beach, Lillian was more like fall, loss and bounty brought together. And so, that last night of the cooking class, after all the other students had cleaned up and headed out, he had resisted their invitations for a nightcap at the local bar and gone back to the restaurant, trying to ignore the sensation that he was still holding Charlie's hand as he opened the gate and walked back up the path to the restaurant kitchen door.

LILLIAN HAD KNOWN, of course. He had told her about Charlie that first night, as they walked around the block, then around the neighborhood, then deep into the city and back, the sky gaining darkness and then light. That first walk she had simply listened, absorbing his story into her. At the end of the night, he had dropped her at her house and paused, uncertain how to say good-bye.

"Substitutions work best in cooking, Tom," she said. Then she kissed him, quietly, and went into the house.

He had stayed away for a while—told himself he had work to do, which was true in many ways. But after a few weeks, he found himself back at the restaurant, sitting at a table by the window. When Lillian had come out into the dining room and seen him, she had walked over to greet him, her hands at her side, and he felt his fingers reaching out to touch hers.

. . .

THEY HAD SPENT the past year together, their lives slowly blending into each other's. They had built trust—of each other, of luck—meal by meal, over a summer spent gathering oysters and clams on the beach, eating dinner in the garden during Lillian's breaks from the restaurant. She told him about her father leaving when she was young, about her mother's death. The way cooking had made life not just better but whole. He told her about growing up on the East Coast, of losing his father, then his wife. Their conversations had wandered into the branches of cherry trees, and finally spread out across bed pillows, words dissolving into touch.

He had forgotten how much a body could desire, how limitless passion could be. After watching a body he loved disintegrate into something he could barely recognize, the glory of the soft curve of Lillian's waist, the line of one long, lean leg escaping from her bathrobe as she sat at the kitchen table in the morning, was almost overwhelming, and he entered her world gratefully and deeply.

"Close your eyes," she would say, and he would feel cashmere against his cheek. "Think jasmine rice.

"And this," she would add, raw silk brushing his chest, "lavender."

And as the fabrics grazed across his skin, he swore he could feel the lines blur between touch and scent, taste and sight and sound.

. . .

WHAT HE HADN'T COUNTED ON, however, was how easily and often other lines would overlap—how he would sometimes hear Charlie's voice as Lillian sang in the shower, how he would see Lillian cooking in his kitchen and remember Charlie coming into the living room, spoon in hand, to get him to taste a new sauce.

Over the months, Lillian's things had slowly been shifting from her apartment to his house. At first only the obvious, the toothbrushes and underwear that made the next day feasible, but eventually, the bits of personality that brought a new color to a bookshelf, a new scent to the couch cushions. Still, he was ridiculously relieved when he found out Lillian preferred the opposite side of the bed to Charlie. It was like driving in England; even if at some point your mind managed to blur the differences in smells and colors and the lilt of an accent—the fact that the cars were driving in the opposite lane could always be counted on to jolt you back to a full recognition of what country you were in.

There was one night, however. Lillian had come home late from the restaurant; Tom was already deeply asleep.

"Slide over," she whispered. "I cricked my neck; I need your side tonight."

Her words came toward him, filtering through dreams of legal briefs and closing arguments. He surfaced only enough to move his body to the right, and then instinctively roll over to cradle her back, his knees sliding into the crook of hers, her head nestled under his chin. Her hair smelled of olive oil and oregano and he inhaled deeply as he slept.

His dreams were golden, incandescent. Stunned by yearning, he reached for her, still half dreaming. She turned toward him, liquid, and it was like entering a river, her body rising and falling against him like a current, her arms and legs wrapped around him. Afterward, he heard her breathing slow and return to sleep; as the first light came through the windows overhead, he lazily opened his eyes and saw her long black hair lying across his chest. Not blond. Not Charlie.

Shaking with guilt, he had gotten out of bed and taken a shower, then gone to work even though it was only five-thirty in the morning. Lillian called him later, her voice still languid, and he told her he was sorry for leaving so early; he had an important case. That evening, when she got home from the restaurant, he massaged her neck for almost an hour, unspoken apologies running through his fingers into her muscles, loosening them. When he was done, she turned, smiling.

"What did I do to deserve you?" she asked.

That night, she slept on her own side of the bed. The day after that, he was assigned a huge case and he dove, thankfully, greedily, into work, where everything had a precedent and all crimes, intentional or not, had a limit on their sentences.

. . .

ISABELLE'S BACK DOOR OPENED and Lillian appeared, wearing his sweater, which hung to her knees, loose as a novice's habit. She looked at him.

"Hey," she said. Her hand touched her stomach.

"When did . . . ?" he asked.

"You know . . ."

And then he realized he did.

"I'm sorry," she said. "I should have . . ."

"No." It was awful that she was apologizing.

"So?"

He looked at her. He realized he'd used all the words already—how long; what did the doctor say. I love you.

"Right," she said, and walked back into the house.

AND THEN THERE WAS NOTHING—just the silence in his house once more, which felt hopelessly, endlessly familiar.

HE WOULD HAVE SLEPT at work, if he could have—although with the hours most associates kept, it wouldn't have made a real difference in how much time he spent there. He was finding sleep overrated in any case, just an unguarded moment for his mind to wander, like a child who can't swim returning again and again to the edge of a pool. So he stayed late, anything to avoid his bed, where he could only lie on his back in the middle, trying to ignore the memories on both sides of him.

Great, he thought, now I have choices.

He worked, throwing hours at the ever hungry case—a complicated high-stakes fight involving a drug company, a young mother, and a fatal side effect. One day his boss caught him as they were leaving a meeting.

"I have another one for you," he said. "You're doing so well with our client here, I thought you might be just the guy for this one. We're her third law firm."

Tom arranged his face into an expression of interested anticipation that had nothing to do with his thoughts. Being the second law firm was not necessarily horrible; in a best-case scenario, it meant that the first firm was incompetent, or that a client's unrealistic expectations had been treated less than sympathetically, which caused the client to leave but hopefully become more malleable going forward. Being the third firm, however, generally meant a client's refusal to let go of a hopeless situation for reasons that had little to do with the jurisprudence. Not for the first time, Tom considered that law school should include more classes on therapy and less time on arcane cases from the 1780s concerning the ownership of goats.

And now, of course, given his "perspective" as a widower, he got all the hopeless ones. Sometimes he felt as if he walked around the office with a sign on his back: GOT GRIEF? Tom wondered what kind of cases he would get if they knew about Lillian.

The new client sat in his office, her hands in her lap, her jaw tight in a way that made Tom's teeth hurt.

"They want me to settle," she said as Tom introduced himself, her words running over his. "Isn't that the strangest word?"

According to the file on Tom's desk, the woman's five-year-old daughter had been killed by a delivery truck when the girl rode her bicycle from their driveway into the rarely traveled cul-de-sac. The driver, a young man, was clearly heartbroken; the company had twice offered settlements that Tom instantly recognized as above the norm.

"I don't want to settle," the woman said.

"What is it you're hoping for?" Tom asked. Likely it was revenge, at this point, but it was always better for clients to hear themselves say it.

"Have you ever lost anyone?" Her stare was direct. Tom knew she didn't believe he had, not if he was sitting there asking her what she wanted.

It was time to switch the focus to her, for him to step gracefully rearward into the position of objective counselor. A shifting of papers. Perhaps an offer of coffee. It wasn't that the law was unfeeling, Tom's boss always said, it just worked better with a little distance. The woman looked at him as if she knew that, too, as if the two of them were standing outside a burning house and people were still inside. As if his refusal to enter was hateful.

"Yes," he said.

She nodded in recognition.

Tom picked up the settlement papers. "The previous offers were generous," he said. "And the young man has apologized. I see here that he wrote you letters."

"Yes."

"What is it you want me to do, then?"

"Make it last longer."

"Why? What is it you hope to accomplish?"

Her hands moved in her lap.

"You need to tell me," he said, "otherwise I can't help you."

"He's the last one who saw her," she said finally.

"And you want him to pay?"

"No." She shook her head and looked at Tom as if perhaps she had been right about him in the beginning. "He and I—we're the last two that saw her. What do I do when he's gone?"

EVEN AS AN ASSOCIATE, he could put in only so many hours at work—at some point he had to go home. Still, there were ways to stall—a nightcap at the bar across the street from the firm, a different and longer route home each night, although it seemed they all eventually led past Lillian's apartment.

One night, as he drove slowly by, he looked up. In the illuminated window he could see Chloe at the sink, washing dishes, Lillian and Isabelle and Al sitting at the table, leaning into each other's words. Tom went home and turned on every light in his house.

"YOU'RE PROBABLY WONDERING why I brought you here."

Isabelle and Tom sat on the front porch of the cabin, looking out over the rocky beach to the water beyond. It was early May, the air still cool, and Isabelle was wrapped up in a blue quilt from one of the beds inside, a red stocking hat on her head. She looked like a determined garden gnome, Tom thought.

"I figure I'm going to get a talking-to," he replied.

"So, are you going to marry her?"

Isabelle's increasing bluntness was a side effect of her "predicament," as she liked to call it—but Tom knew that she was not above using it for her own purposes, either. It was one of the things he liked most about her, when he stopped to think about it.

"So much for subtlety," he replied with a wry smile.

"The woman is getting round," Isabelle said.

Tom wondered sometimes how people kept moving forward into things like marriage and children. He and Isabelle both knew what it felt like to watch a spouse leave you. Divorce or death; in either case you were left with half a contract, riveted in place by promises you had not broken. You could try to move—forward, sideways—but in the end it seemed you were always traveling in a circle, coming back to the moment of departure. No wonder they gave out rings at the ceremony.

"I don't know how to do it," Tom said.

"Maybe you need a different 'it,' dear," Isabelle commented, tugging her hat down over the top of her ears.

"But while you're here," she added casually, "there is something you could do for me."

TOM STOOD LOOKING at the hunks of wood—a half-cord, easily, he figured, although the logs he had chopped in his teenage years had been clean, consistent lengths, redolent with the smells of alder and maple, their bright surfaces almost begging to be cut. He remembered the joy of his growing muscles, the loft of the axe as it swung up in an endless arc and then came slamming down. The complete and utter satisfaction of a smooth surface cleaving into air as the pieces went flying to either side of him.

This was not going to be like that, he could tell, looking at the haphazard jumble of gnarled stumps and logs, half of it wet and rotting, the other portion hard and glistening and green. This was wood that defied the axe, a living lesson that when it came to heat, sometimes it was better to use man's other inventions—electricity, gas, propane.

"Where did you get this?" he asked Isabelle.

"My neighbors did some land-clearing," she said innocently. "Wasn't it nice of them?"

Isabelle had had the cabin for decades, Tom knew. She'd heated with wood for the years she lived there; she'd even bragged to him about chopping her own supply. Isabelle knew junk wood when she saw it.

"Isabelle," he said. "Be reasonable."

"Being reasonable never taught me anything," Isabelle responded calmly. "Nor will it keep my cabin warm. I'll be inside if you need me."

TOM HADN'T PICKED UP an axe in almost fifteen years, not since his father died and his family stopped going to the lake. Tom centered the first hunk on the flattest piece of ground he could find, hoping for muscle memory, or at least muscles. He had chosen a rotten piece, figuring it would be an easy start. He held the axe level, feeling the balance, the weight of its head in his right hand, his left cradling the curve of the grip. He remembered his father giving him a lesson, watching his father's arms heave the axe up, right hand sliding down the wooden belly to meet the left, bent knees straightening, his body lifting up, almost off the ground.

"Gravity is your friend," he told Tom.

Now Tom hoisted the axe above his head, hearing the sounds of his right hand sliding down the handle, the blade moving through the air. He felt gravity grab the axe head as it reached the top of its arc, and he brought it down, feeling it enter the log with a soft, soggy thud. He rocked the handle back and forth and the wood collapsed sleepily into pieces, insects skittering for cover, fat white larvae curling up against the light.

He laid the pieces out in the sun, shaking his head.

It took him an hour to get through the water-softened hunks, but by the last one he was feeling masterful. The axe swung in a smooth, intuitive arc; the logs fell apart almost before the blade touched them. It would be months if not years before they would be any good for burning, but, at least, separated into pieces and stacked out of the rain, they would have a head start on drying. It felt good to do something physical, to feel as if he was being useful in a way you could measure by height or weight.

He shifted his attention to the other half of the pile and manhandled one of its gnarled chunks into place. It sat there, squat and irritated, its rings swirling out of line, pushed into new shapes by limbs that had started forming early on.

The axe blade plummeted down, bouncing off the implacable surface of the log and careening toward his leg.

"Shit!" he yelled, leaping back.

Isabelle poked her head out the door of the cabin, a white bowl ringed with painted blue flowers in her hands. The picture of tidy domesticity.

"Everything all right out there?" she asked.

"Thrill a minute," he said.

"Look at all that you've done," she noted. "You'll be finished in no time."

The door closed.

Tom glared at the door, then at the log that sat unmarked by the experience.

He flexed his thumbs, feeling the blisters that were already forming. He hoisted the axe, hearing his muscles growl, then brought it down hard and straight, feeling it connect with a jolt that blasted up his arms and lodged in his jaw. When he looked down, he saw a thin crack in the wood—a paper cut, at most. He pulled the axe out easily and aimed again for the same spot. Again. And again, his arms pounding with blood. Finally, he felt the blade sink in, but when he tried to pull it out again, it wouldn't come. He rocked the handle from side to side. Nothing. He lifted the axe and the log came with it, hanging there like a dead thing.

The muscles in his arms were shaking. He had made a mistake—he should have done this pile first, while he was still fresh. He was too tired for this. Glancing up at the cabin, he could see Isabelle through the window, putting on a kettle for tea. Scotch would have been better, he thought. She looked out, a wave morphing into a thumbs-up.

Fine.

Still holding the handle, he slammed the log into the ground, hoping to wedge the axe in deeper, or remove it, or something.

"Let go," he muttered between his teeth, as he raised and then battered the log at the end of the axe. "Let GO." It didn't release, but slowly he could feel the blade moving inward, an inch or so each time, until finally the log split into two pieces.

"YES!" he yelled triumphantly.

He looked around at the pile next to him. There were still twenty-five logs left—and Isabelle's patience appeared to be endless.

SOMEWHERE AROUND log number ten he ceased to care. His body took over, the endless bass beat of the axe pummeling his mind into numbness. Log after log after log.

You got to the point where you believed that was all life was, just one piece of bad news after another—a test result, a failed medication, a nurse's sympathetic expression, stupefying you, claiming space in your brain that used to house memories of your wife's naked body running into the ocean, of the grin on her face as she lifted a brush to paint your bedroom walls a warm and luscious apricot that you swore to her you'd never like.

What had made him believe he could love Lillian after

that? She had said she didn't believe in substitutions. She had opened a door and he had walked through, grateful. But he had only half entered, bringing all of that with him.

He could feel it as he chopped—the deep, black anger, the grief crammed between his shoulder blades like chunks of dirty, compacted ice. He raised the axe and aimed for the gnarled stump in front of him. His swing ramped up to a staccato, his muscles screaming. It wasn't until he couldn't see the log in front of him that he realized he was crying.

He put down the axe and sat on the ground. His skin steamed, sending clouds of heat up into the cool air. He was tired, empty. Spent, his father always used to say—as if energy was something you might have saved if you'd been careful, thinking of the future. Something neither of them had had, in the end, Tom thought. Although as he sat there, his body thrumming, Tom understood that wasn't true in his case. He had a future, but he had been no better than the mother in his office, their minds locked into immobility with the effort of looking back, remembering not what they'd had but the loss of it.

"They aren't leftovers," Charlie used to tell him as she took the bits and pieces of a previous day's meal out of the refrigerator. "They're a head start."

Tom looked at the cut logs scattered around him. He shifted his shoulders, stood up, and started stacking them.

. . .

"HERE," ISABELLE SAID, coming up next to him as he put the last log in place. She handed him a beer. "Why don't you take this down to the beach?"

Tom walked to the edge of the water, his body shivering from exertion. His rational mind noted that tomorrow was likely going to hurt. He put on his sweatshirt and lowered himself carefully onto a driftwood log, looking down Isabelle's inlet toward the bay. Back at the cabin was a stack of cut wood, almost as tall as he was. At his feet he could hear the tide, running through the stones as it moved up the beach. He felt the smoothness of the log under his legs, the breeze cooling the sweat in his hair. He wanted to sit there and never leave.

When Tom was young, his family used to go to a lake in Vermont every summer for two weeks. They would arrive, Tom blasting out of a car that had become stifling during the last few miles, as his father drove with the windows rolled up against the dust of the dirt road. And there it would be, a circle of blue surrounded by trees, the air suddenly, startlingly clear. Cousins and summer friends would come out of the cabins and run down the steps and they would all disappear into a world of cattails and rowboats, wooden docks and cannonballs into early morning water so cold it stole your breath.

Over the years, those two weeks had served as chapter headings in his life. His first broken bone (arm, rope swing). His first fish (trout, slamming about in the bottom of the boat, anger coloring the taste of its meat; he would try it later that evening and never eat trout again). His first sighting of a female breast (his older sister's friend, whose bikini top had miraculously disengaged in a dive into the water, allowing a stunningly generous portion of flesh, a shell-pink nipple, to appear for a moment before she dunked, with a scream, below the surface). His first sexual experience (sixteen; Julianne from the next cabin over). The only time his father had sent him home (see above). The first time he beat his aunt at poker. The last time he saw his grandfather—the chapters over time creating a coherent plot line for his life.

For some reason, everything seemed so much clearer when he was at the lake. Tom had tried to talk about it once to his father, who had misunderstood and gone on a long tangent about weather patterns and a lack of pollution. But that hadn't been what Tom meant. For Tom, life in the city was full of patterns so complex you could never see the separate strands. But the cabin never changed; it was the place he returned to, judged his own progress against its sameness—the unexpectedly tall top porch step that tripped him as a toddler later becoming a comfortable resting spot for his long teenage legs as he sat on a Fourth of July watching the fireworks. When he returned after his freshman year in college, he came to see that porch step as a joke played on every newcomer, whose eventual instinctive adjustment to its height would be a sign of their true inclusion in the tribe of summer people.

The cabin had held the shape and color of his childhood, had given a wholeness to the intricate relationships that were his family. Tom wondered now, if his father hadn't died and the lake tradition with him, would Tom have completed a circle, returned and seen the porch step with the eyes of a father, worried that his own toddler would trip?

Behind him, Tom heard Isabelle picking her way along the rocks toward the water. She came up and put her hand on his shoulder.

"Feeling better?" she asked.

Tom took a long, steady drink from the beer bottle.

"Isabelle," he said, as he put it down on the driftwood log, "I think I know what we should do."

"YOU MUST HAVE BALLS the size of Georgia peaches."

Chloe stood in the restaurant kitchen doorway. Tom could see the after-lunch cleanup going on behind her, but no Lillian in sight.

"Chloe," he began.

"We trusted you. With Lillian. Do you remember what that means around here?"

"Would you just let me try?"

Finnegan came up behind Chloe.

"Chloe," he said. "Lillian doesn't need a guard dog."

"I don't either," Chloe snapped.

"Okay, then." Lillian said as she approached, wiping her hands on her apron. She was beautiful, Tom thought.

"Back to work, you two," Lillian directed Chloe and Finnegan. She stepped outside, closing the door, bringing the smell of lemons with her. Tom could feel in his bones how much he wanted to be part of the clear, citrus world in front of him.

"They really need to figure that out," Lillian said, gazing over her shoulder toward the kitchen.

"Would you come with me?" Tom said. "There's something I'd like to show you."

She turned to look at him. "We've done this before," she commented.

"There are three of us now."

"There were three of us then." Her voice was sad but firm. Lillian the teacher, the girlfriend, had always been calm and understanding, her insights a river you could flow into, float down, knowing you would be taken care of. This new Lillian's river had muscle, a destination. Life on this water would require different skills, but you'd get somewhere, he understood as he looked at her.

"Yes," he said. "Different three."

She nodded, and went inside, closing the door behind her. Tom thought that might be it, that she was gone, or at best he would have to wait until the dishes were washed, the last of the leftovers covered and set on the shelves in the walk-in refrigerator. But then she stepped out, a jacket around her shoulders.

THEY DROVE FOR AN HOUR, the car silent. Tom could feel the words jostling about inside him, wanting to come out, but they all felt tainted by the things he hadn't said. Two months ago she had offered him the gift of herself, of the baby, and all he had done was look for the price tag, to see how many memories it would cost him. So now he matched her quiet as they drove along the highway, then onto a winding two-lane road, and finally down a long tree-lined lane to where it ended and opened at the edge of a bay.

Lillian looked at him appraisingly, but Tom just got out and pulled two paddles, a blanket, and a cushioned seat pad from the trunk and walked over to a red canoe that lay on its side, locked to an evergreen tree. Lillian got out and watched as he took a key from his pocket and undid the canoe, pulling it down to the rocky shore and placing the cushion on the bow seat.

"Can I ask where we're going?" Her hand resting on her stomach.

"Not far. It'll be safe; I grew up doing this, remember?"

"That was a lake, in the summer. The water was a bit warmer." But he saw a smile swimming below the surface of her expression. He knew she was remembering—a late morning in her apartment, Federico sautéing trout in the restaurant below. Tom lying next to her, telling her about trying not to catch fish as his father pretended not to notice. She had relaxed into the stories of his childhood and they had opened to let her in.

"We'll stay close to the shore," he said.

SHE SAT IN THE FRONT of the canoe, her back to him, the green-and-black-plaid blanket across her lap, the paddle resting lightly in her hands. The water was quiet around them, the ink-dark evergreen trees rising up on the hills around the bay. Tom's paddle met the water, sliding back, pushing the canoe forward. On the second stroke, Lillian's did the same. Tom angled his blade to steer their course, keeping to the shallows where they could look down and see the rocks that would later, at low tide, be dried by the evening air.

Tom looked at the straight line of Lillian's back, the movement of her arms, strong from years of mixing and kneading. He could just see the rounding of her stomach as she shifted her body into each stroke. The canoe rocked gently, and Tom wondered if the baby could feel the motion. He wondered if a baby that had spent its gestation on the water would love boats later, or perhaps simply come into the world believing it was as peaceful as everything that had come before. It would be nice to think so.

They rounded a finger of land that stretched out into the bay, creating an inlet on the other side. At its head was a single cabin, the lights on.

Tom steered the canoe down the inlet; Lillian turned her head and gazed over her shoulder at him, questioning.

"It's ours," Tom said, letting his paddle rest across his knees.

"Just us," he added. Lillian looked at him more closely.

"Well, almost," he said, embarrassment running through his voice. "I mean, I did promise her visitation rights."

"Who?"

"Isabelle."

Lillian's smile spread slowly across her face.

"Might there be a bed in that cabin?" she asked.

"Yes."

"Good," she said. "Paddle on."

The

NOTEBOOKS

Finnegan Short had grown past his name by the age of six, muscles and bones racing in a sprint to his eventual six-foot, seven-inch height. By the time he was eight years old, he had stretched into the world of adults. He would try to play with children his own age, folding his legs like an origami crane, curling his spine, lowering his head. But it was never quite enough. It didn't matter how excited he got, whether he used the same vocabulary as all his friends or crashed his Hot Wheels cars with equal enthusiasm—there was something that happened when his long fingers reached out to fix the racetrack that was laid across his friend's living room floor, when he extended a seemingly endless arm to catch his car before it skittered under a couch. Whatever his actions, the body he did them with screamed grown-up, invader. His only option was to go where his height dictated.

Finnegan's parents were mountain climbers; at night, they told their son stories of mountains in foreign lands, about the decreasing amount of oxygen in the air as you ascended, the way it affected your heart and clarity of thought. It made sense to him; there was a straightforwardness to life lived down among children that disappeared in the altitude of grown-ups. In the upper climes of maturity, Finnegan found, the issues were the same as where he came from—a desire not to share, a burst of love or hate, an overwhelming sense of fear or anger or despair—but with adults, it was as if they were talking through oxygen masks; you had to concentrate hard to understand what they were really saying.

Which was perhaps why Finnegan began to listen so carefully to the conversations of grown-ups. If he was quiet enough, he could observe unnoticed; the irony was that while his height made him obvious to children, his youth made him invisible to adults. From his vantage point he learned the rules of their interactions, saw how the language that ran underneath their words tended to hold the meaning. The drop of a gaze, the pulling back of a foot, the leaning forward of a chin. The hugs that weren't hugs, just shoulders meeting, hands patting backs in silent, mutual applause. Sometimes Finnegan wondered why adults used words at all. Some days words seemed more like clothes, created to distract attention from things you didn't want other people to notice.

Finnegan's parents were an exception, however. Perhaps it was all the ascents they had done, inuring them to the effects of thinner air, strengthening the muscles of their hearts; perhaps, Finnegan would think, years later, it was the simple fact of facing death more often than others that made them approach life with such joyful honesty. All Finnegan knew, and all he wanted to know, was that he was loved without question.

DURING HIS CHILDHOOD, there were only a few places where Finnegan did not feel tall, but one of them was his home. Finnegan's parents ran a climbing-gear company in Boulder, Colorado, and their house was an extension of their business, the ceiling in the living room reaching twenty feet into the air, one wall lined with windows, the opposite side set up with climbing routes. Almost as soon as he could walk, Finnegan found himself in a harness, heading upward. He never had the heart to tell his parents that he was scared of heights, that even his own altitude was almost more than he could bear—that the best part of climbing, the only part that made him continue, was the feeling of their arms around him when he landed back on the ground. For that, he would go as high as they wanted him to.

Afterward, they would sit on a blanket on the wide-plank wooden floor of the living room, eating peanut butter sandwiches and drinking milk or coffee from blue metal camping cups, and his mother would talk about the mental puzzle of making your way up a difficult wall or how miraculous it felt to have the tips of your fingers and toes holding up the weight of your body. On Saturday nights, they would set up a tent in the middle of the living room and his father would tell tales of fearless climbers and evenings in base camps, of the way a lamp could light up the inside of a tent and make it feel like home in the midst, or perhaps because of, the wind and the cold outside.

Unlike his parents, Finnegan was not fearless, and the thought of ever losing them felt like a hole where his lungs used to be. When his mother or father was off climbing a mountain, he would replay their stories in his head, but there were never enough to make up for the absence. At the next picnic in the living room, he would clamor for more, fingering the climbing-chalk bag attached to his belt, pretending that he was putting the stories in there, where they would always be safe and close to him.

After Finnegan's birth, his parents had agreed they would no longer climb mountains together, one of them always staying behind. But when Finnegan was fourteen, they were offered an opportunity to climb Everest. They gazed at their son, by that time taller than either of them, his face showing the early signs of a mustache, and accepted. It had been so long, and look, there was Finn, as grown-up as anyone you could imagine. The storm that swept their base camp and stranded his parents beyond the reach of help was heralded as a great tragedy for the mountaineering community.

Finnegan refused to comment when the press, hungry for the emotional story in the orphaning of a freakishly tall adolescent—How would he ever fit into life without the guidance of his parents? What did he think of their leaving him? Would he ever be able to forgive them?—rang the doorbell and took pictures through the giant living room window. They waited outside the house for days without ever catching a glimpse of the boy-man they sought.

The neighbors, who had promised Finnegan's parents to keep an eye on their son while they were on Everest, were overwhelmed by caretaking of this magnitude. It was Finnegan's father's sister who arrived and took over, chasing the reporters away with a vocabulary worthy of a shipful of sailors.

"We're the only two left of our tribe," she told him after the last reporter was gone from the front lawn and she had shut the door. "All the rest went and got themselves killed.

"Sorry," she added. "I'm not really used to being around people. Your dad always said I was missing the filter on my brain."

She was shorter than Finnegan and had to crane her head back to see into his eyes, but she did just that.

"Do you want some scrambled eggs for dinner?" she asked. "I can't really cook, but I can do that."

AUNT AILIS WAS A technical writer for a software company in Portland, Oregon. She was as wide as Finnegan's father had been wiry, loud where he had been contemplative. And she definitely was missing her filter. She said what she thought—sometimes, it seemed to Finnegan, before she thought it, her comments flying so fast and far beyond social convention that he caught himself looking for their jet trails.

"For Christ's sake," she told the funeral director who came by to offer his services, "what would we need a coffin for? His parents are popsicles. And when their bodies are found, they'll be burned."

Finnegan could see the reactions on people's faces, the shock they quickly tried to hide when Aunt Ailis would make one of her comments. They saw his aunt as someone devoid of sensitivity; he knew by the way their hands would flutter in his direction, as if trying to shoo her words away from him. They would change the subject, talk about flower arrangements, grief counselors, the solace of knowing someone you loved died doing something that brought them joy, talking in their smooth, soothing voices, so much like vanilla pudding that Finnegan wondered if they had to be refrigerated at night.

They thought he should be taken away from her, he could see that, too, in the way their shoulders inclined toward him, but not so much as to take responsibility for doing anything about it. He was glad of the latter part. In an odd way, it was a relief being with Aunt Ailis. She said what she thought, her body mirroring her words. She didn't expect him to agree with her, or even want him to, for that matter; it was obvious she had given up on the idea of anyone doing that years ago. As a result, Finnegan felt his own mind open and walk about, finding its way into thoughts that felt real or true or good to him.

"Your parents were idiots," Aunt Ailis had said that first night at Finnegan's house. "What were they thinking?"

She looked at him over the plate of scrambled eggs.

"But they loved you. How can you fit both those things in one mind? I wish there was a way we could look in people's brains and see how they do it."

Finnegan nodded. He wondered what his own brain would look like now if someone scanned it, whether grief would be green, anger red, fear a neon orange. Or maybe the colors wouldn't stay separated; maybe that's how all the emotions fit in one brain, and it was only people who needed to compartmentalize them. Maybe it was okay to be sad and scared and angry and lonely all at the same time—if he could be all those things without having to choose, then maybe his parents could have left him and loved him without choosing, either.

Aunt Ailis took Finnegan with her when she went home to Portland. She asked him if he wanted to keep his parents' house, for later. He looked at the walls, the grips, the ropes, and said no. So they sold it to a retired circus performer, who happily told them that he planned to re-create the big top within the high walls of the living room. Finnegan thought his parents would have liked the idea of their house turned into a giant red-and-white-striped tent, filled with dreams of trapezes and elephants and the occasional clown, all of them together, sheltered against the cold and the wind.

BOULDER HAD FELT like a wide-rimmed teacup, held in the benevolent hands of the mountains that surrounded it. Portland was more like a game of hide-and-seek, a city nesting at an intersection of rivers and roads, covered by bridges and rain clouds. Finnegan missed the big, wide sky of Boulder, the way the thinner air seemed to require more space, spreading out blue and clean. At Aunt Ailis's house, which sat a scant eighty-three feet above sea level, the air was thick and rich and green; it made his lungs heavy.

Finnegan told his aunt he was a runner, although that had never been true before. Running seemed the only way he could bring back the slightly breathless feeling of his childhood. He dug through his boxes and found an old pair of tennis shoes and set off early in the mornings. His long legs took him far from Aunt Ailis's house, but she never commented, just replaced one pair of shoes with another as he wore through them. He ran through that first summer, his stride lengthening with the days, taking him along rivers and into rambling parks with trees that towered over his head and made him feel, finally, small. In the fall, he ran after school and even though the cross-country coach approached him, he preferred to be by himself, if for no other reason than the team never ran far enough to get him past the weight of his own lungs.

He ran his way around lakes and up hills and through the canyons of downtown buildings, through the end of middle school and into high school. Aunt Ailis said some people just took longer to acclimate.

A COUPLE OF BLOCKS from Aunt Ailis's house was an old, decrepit relic of a house. Its once-white paint was peeling off the wooden siding, the windows were covered by red curtains now faded to pink by the sun, which must have taken decades, Finnegan thought, considering how little the sun ever seemed to find its way to the Pacific Northwest. The garden was wild, untended, a rummage sale of rhododendrons and dandelions. Finnegan had seen evidence that someone lived there—a newly delivered telephone book disappearing from the front porch, although not immediately; a light at night behind the heavy curtains upstairs. There was much speculation among the neighbors, but not a one of them had had any contact with the inhabitant over the past ten years.

And then, one autumn day some four years after he moved to Portland, Finnegan went by the house on his way to school and saw an ambulance in front, two men carrying out a frail woman on a stretcher. Not covered; he could see her face, her eyes looking around her with a kind of marvel in them. The paramedics put the woman into the ambulance and shut the doors, and Finnegan went on to school, thinking.

There was no sign of habitation for weeks after that. Rumor traveled around the neighborhood; it seemed that once the door to the house had been opened, news followed. The woman, it turned out, had been moved to an assisted-living facility after the hospital. Her name was Maridel House, an appropriate surname for someone who was known for nothing other than the residence she lived in.

Every day, Finnegan walked by the House house, and every day his steps took him a bit closer—to the edge of the sidewalk, then onto the front lawn, where the tall grass soaked his shoes and left his socks damp for the rest of the day. By the second week, he had ventured as far as the porch; by the third, he was trying windows, the back and basement doors, one each day—a game of roulette.

It wasn't about the act of entry itself, he knew that much; what he wanted was to be inside, which was altogether different. He also knew, of course, that he shouldn't—and thus the slow courting, the daily request. If the house wanted him, it would accept him, grant him access. By the end of the third week, when he tried the last basement window and it opened, it didn't feel like breaking and entering at all.

He went in feet first, carefully lowering himself to the uncertain ground below him, then made his way through the darkened room, eventually finding the stairs and then the kitchen above, which was surprisingly neat and clean, as if the owner had been preparing for company instead of paramedics. He wandered into the living room. He didn't know what he expected to find—the closed curtains and reclusive nature of the inhabitant should have led him toward theories of hoarding, and yet, he had never thought that about the house. It had always felt full, but not physically.

He pushed open a curtain a bit for light and made his way around the room, stopping at the fireplace mantel before a line of six framed photographs. A sepia print of a man in theatrical makeup and garb; a mother and three young children, the picture equally old. And then the rest, moving through time: two girls, then women, then crones.

He reached out, without thinking, and took the picture of the two old women, slipping it inside his jacket. Outside, he heard the honk of a car and remembered suddenly that he was late for school. He started for the front door, the quickest way out. As he opened it, he heard, too late, the sound of footsteps on the front porch, and then saw the startled face of the local real estate agent.

"WELL, that was just stupid," Aunt Ailis said, shaking her head.

Finnegan nodded, the flush of mortification rolling down the long length of his body.

"They aren't going to charge you with anything, but that doesn't mean we're done. If you're going to take things, you have to learn to take something that people need to give."

She pulled out a box from her overstuffed hall closet. Inside were stacks of blue exam books.

"I taught a class at the community college," Aunt Ailis said, by way of explanation. Finnegan could tell by the way her hands lingered as she picked up one of the blue books that her tenure at the college had not been as long as she would have liked.

"Here," she said. "You might as well use one of these. They're just going to waste."

"What am I going to use it for?" he asked.

"You'll see," she answered.

Which is how Finnegan ended up, the next Saturday afternoon, in Maridel House's tiny room in the assisted-living center, a blue notebook in his lap and a pen in his hand.

"SO, YOU LIKE MY HOUSE?" Maridel looked at him, her eyes green as river water.

"You could have knocked, before," she commented. "When I lived there. I would have answered the door."

Finnegan nodded. He wanted to disagree, tell her that everything about the house, from its overrun garden to the buckling front walk and the mailbox that tilted across it, seemed to be there for the sole purpose of keeping people away. Even the wooden siding appeared to recoil from the paint that had been applied to its surface. But he realized that might not sound very polite, and would certainly throw more suspicion on why he had wanted so badly to be inside in the first place. And, as he didn't really know why he had, it seemed easier to avoid the topic.

"I've lived there my whole life," Maridel said. "This is my first time away. The nurse says to think of it as a vacation."

Maridel looked around her, at the flat white walls of her room. "I wonder where she goes for fun," she remarked. "I always kind of thought that if I went anywhere, it would be to Greece. Or Rome. Or maybe go to see kangaroos in Africa."

She gazed blandly at Finnegan, then more sharply.

"You can correct me," she said. "I don't break."

He looked up and saw her eyes on him, watching.

"Or you can get me a glass of water," she added.

"I AM THE HOLDER of my family's stories," Maridel said. Her hands, crabbed by arthritis, rested in two half-circles around the water glass on the small table in front of her. "There is nobody left but me."

Finnegan observed the old woman in front of him. Her frailness stunned him, her hair almost shimmering in its lack of color, her skin so thin he wondered how it could hold the blood and bones inside. He wondered, too, what would happen to her stories when their container failed, as hers surely would. He thought of her stories slipping out of the rubble left behind, traveling on currents of wind, separating into particles. Would they float out there, or would they simply drop silently onto the earth, into the ocean?

The thought filled him with a strange sense of despair. Finnegan opened his blue notebook and raised his pen. "Tell me," he said simply, and then, remembering his aunt's admonitions, he added, "please."

FOR SUCH A SMALL CONTAINER, Maridel seemed to hold a tremendous number of stories.

"I was the oldest," Maridel told Finnegan. "Fourteen when our mother died of the influenza in 1926. My father was an actor, all mustache and capes, always entering the front door as if he was arriving onstage. I still remember him coming out of my mother's room that night she died. He said she was made to be a parent, but he wasn't. He handed me twenty dollars and left. For a while we hoped he was coming back, but then we realized he wasn't. My twelve-year-old brother said he wasn't going to stick around if I was in charge, so that left my sister and my little brother, who was two years old then. He was killed by a car a few years later, and so then it was just my sister and me."

Finnegan watched Maridel counting, polishing the losses of her life as if they were beads on a rosary.

"We wouldn't have made it without the neighbors," she continued. "They dropped off food and hired me to do sewing and mending. They always paid me too much, even though nobody had anything extra to spare back then. And they always seemed to know when the social workers were going to come checking on us. A neighbor who was the local butcher would drop off a piece of meat, and I'd get cooking. All it ever took was a pot roast. If the social worker walked in to that smell coming from the oven, they never asked us about our parents. So we got to stay together."

The outline of Maridel's life was quickly sketched that

first evening, but even then, Finnegan could see that what she had told him was like a blueprint of a house waiting to be built, the most important details merely suggested by its basic lines. It took a single sentence for Maridel to explain that she and her sister had lived together in the house until Hattie had died a few years ago. A short string of words holding almost eight decades of moments—a hand passing a freshly washed plate to a sister standing with a drying towel, the swirl of a skirt, the celebration of a new job, men who entered their lives but never the front door. A cat that Hattie had wanted. An argument over the paint color for the house. Finnegan could hear Maridel's voice change as she talked about her sister's death, the way the sounds echoed and became an empty room. He understood what that felt like. He sat, populating the page with her words.

AUNT AILIS HAD COMMENTED after a few weeks that he could stop going to the nursing home whenever he wished, but he found he didn't wish. Every Tuesday and Thursday he would jog to the nursing home, keeping his stride easy so he wouldn't arrive in a sweat. It was a two-mile run, not hard. The first mile he spent letting go of the day, the jokes the other kids made about human skyscrapers, the curious glances as he tried to fit his body under the showerhead in the locker room. By the time he was into mile two, the evening was opening up before him and the lights of the nursing home were soon reaching out to greet him.

He found he enjoyed his time with Maridel. After her house sold, she had asked Finnegan to bring her the blue and orange and yellow scarves from her bureau drawer and then directed him in hanging them from the ceiling of her room in great swaths.

"We can pretend we are nomads," she said. "And this is our tent. It'll be our vacation."

He had spent the winter in the gold-and-orange glow of her room, listening. His run home was always faster, his feet flying on the wet pavement, the streetlights illuminating the world in shimmering circles.

By the end of March, Finnegan had filled three blue notebooks, but he didn't stop. After Maridel came Luanne, down the hall, and then Simon and Jasper. Simon and Jasper lived in another nursing home, but Maridel had met them at a senior-citizen dance years before and she said Finnegan should talk to them.

"They have no families," Maridel explained. "And Simon was a railroad man; he has lots of tales to tell. They shouldn't be lost."

Simon and Jasper led to Viola and Ida. Henriette. Hannah. Voices strong or wavering, shaking out their stories like bedsheets fresh from the dryer. Regrets and anger and small moments of pure joy. A starched yellow dress from childhood. A lost engagement ring, found years later in a picnic basket. The first, or last, sight of a child. A rosebush, dug up and moved from one house to another. A kiss that shouldn't have happened. The pages filled and Finnegan paid less and less attention to high school, until suddenly it was over and he was out on the other side, barely, his head full of other people's lives.

OVER THE YEARS, Aunt Ailis had tried to lure Finnegan into the world of computers, the lines of software code that she studied as if they would give her a key to the inner workings of the human brain, if not heart. Finnegan understood the satisfaction she derived from the act of coding, her ability to aim for and achieve something she already knew she wanted—but for Finnegan, his interest in people's stories was always the unexpected memories that lingered beneath the words, waiting to come out. As far as Finnegan could understand, the purpose of coding was to create a form of stable perfection, a series of commands that could reproduce every time exactly what was intended. The opposite of humans, who were interesting to Finnegan precisely because of the way their narratives changed, hid other meanings, shifted with time and perspective.

So he reached out and took the stories in, knowing they had nowhere else to go, unable to refuse safe haven to memories that otherwise would disappear unnoticed. And yet, at times he was overwhelmed by the weight of other people's lives, the stacks of notebooks that surrounded his bed.

"You could publish them," Aunt Ailis suggested. But Finnegan knew, somehow, that wasn't the answer. What he had experienced in the transfer of these stories was as intimate as touch, a table for two in a crowded restaurant. It didn't seem right for them to be made public. Still, he didn't know what to do with them, didn't know who he was without them.

And so he sat in his room, surrounded. Over the months he stopped opening his window shades; he gave up running. He avoided the nursing home, with its rooms full of tales wanting to be told. He sat on his bed and picked up one notebook after another, reading.

"YOU NEED TO figure this out," Aunt Ailis said, some five months after Finnegan's high school graduation. "And it's becoming apparent that's not going to happen here."

She hugged him, once, fast, and then handed him the keys to her old Honda Civic. "A present," she said. "Now, go."

THE INTERSTATE THAT CURVED its way through downtown Portland was otherwise long and mostly straight, running the entire length of the western coast of the United States. From Portland, Finnegan could head south and drive for days and days without ever leaving the highway, all the way to Mexico, into sunshine and bright colors and languages he didn't speak. Even if people wanted to tell him stories, he wouldn't be able to understand.

If he turned north, it was only a matter of six hours or so to Canada, through landscape that he believed would feel familiar, green and blue, mountains and water. In Canada, most people would speak his language, but he had heard Canadians didn't think all that highly of Americans, so it was unlikely they would see him as a worthy recipient of their narratives.

He sat, his car idling, at the overpass above I-5. In the trunk of the Civic was a big box of blue notebooks; the backseat held three paper bags of clothes and a pair of running shoes that Aunt Ailis had thrown in at the last minute. He looked south and saw traffic heading out of Portland, cars jammed against each other like spawning salmon. He clicked on the left-turn indicator and aimed for Canada.

STOMACH AND GAS TANK both hit empty four hours north. Finnegan took an exit, hoping for a gas station and food that had never been inside a hermetically sealed package. After months of living in his head, he had started seeing colors again as he drove along the highway—the yellow of an outsized Hummer muscling its way up the fast lane, the inky green of the pine trees lining the road. He could feel the slip of the steering wheel under his fingertips, smell how the air changed as he passed a river, a diesel car, a burger joint. While usually a road trip lulled him to sleep, this one seemed to be having exactly the opposite effect. He found himself wanting food, real food, the kind that would require him to use two hands and taste buds.

As he filled the gas tank, he spotted a fruit-and-vegetable stand across the street, and, more important, the young woman who was holding up a shining red apple and laughing with the vendor. She was about his age, her hair dark and curling, her height just tall enough to reach the vendor's shoulder. Finnegan couldn't have told you what it was about her; all he knew was that he felt as if he might have room for one more story if it was hers. When he saw her leave on foot, he quickly topped off his tank and parked his car on the street, then followed her at a discreet distance past a small hardware store, a bagel shop, a bookstore, a dust-covered window cluttered with old couches and swatches of faded fabric. He wondered where she could be going with her bag of apples, or what she would think if he stretched out his stride and caught up with her.

This was so unlike him—he who had spent his junior and senior prom nights in nursing homes—that he never stopped to consider his actions. And when she finally reached an iron gate that opened to a restaurant and walked down a side path that led to what he could only assume was the kitchen, he simply stopped and waited, despite the aromas coming from inside, a scent that felt like stories that knew where they belonged. As much as he wanted to enter the restaurant, sit at a table and eat for days, he didn't want to risk the chance that she might walk back out while he wasn't there.

It was November. Rain was coming, he could sense it in the way the air was getting heavier about him. He had always liked to run at times like these; he enjoyed the idea of racing the raindrops to his own door. Standing was not nearly as fun, and as the first drops fell he had almost decided to give up when the kitchen door opened yet again and a man in his mid-thirties, a bloody dishtowel wrapped around his hand and a torrent of Spanish coming from his mouth, came quickly down the path.

As Finnegan was opening the gate for the man, he looked up and saw the girl standing in the kitchen doorway, an apron around her waist and her arms crossed in frustration. Finnegan walked through the open gate and approached.

"Can I help?" he asked.

"I don't know," she said. "Can you wash dishes?"

WHICH IS ALL SHE HAD SAID to him for the first six weeks he worked at Lillian's. Her name, he found out, was Chloe, and she worked longer and harder hours than even Lillian, coming in early or staying late to try new recipes. Finnegan watched her when he could get away with it, catching a glimpse between stacks of dishes. What he saw when she cooked was equal parts desire to please Lillian and a love for the food itself—sentiments he could well understand, but he wondered when the latter would tip the scale and Chloe would cook for herself.

It was a story worth waiting for, he decided, and after the first few nights in a less than attractive motel, Finnegan found himself a room in a house he shared with five computer science students, who made for occasionally odd but, after Aunt Ailis's social quirks, reasonably familiar roommates. Finnegan ate at the restaurant, so he could avoid the kitchen at home, with its towers of pizza boxes and silver Top Ramen flavor packets, the overflowing sink of dishes that he might have felt a professional obligation to wash. At the end of the first month, he bought himself a futon, then a lamp. A secondhand dresser for his clothes. The box of notebooks stayed in the trunk of his car.

He started running again in the mornings before work. He wouldn't admit that he was hoping to catch sight of where Chloe lived, but the possibility took him farther and deeper into the city, down serpentine streets lined with trees, over hills to neighborhoods of small bungalows snuggled into perfect grids. He never saw her, but he saw enough of the city to know he was comfortable there, where drivers stopped their cars to allow him to cross the street, and running in the rain or the semi-light of early morning was not a solitary occupation. As he ran, he tried to think of things he could say to Chloe. A cooking tip from one of the books he was reading. A comment about the way the color of her hair matched the batter for Lillian's signature chocolate cake. He could say he was collecting stories and ask for hers—but what had sounded sincere with the senior citizens just sounded smarmy when he thought of saying it to a girl his own age. And so he stayed at the restaurant kitchen sink, his back to the cooks, his ears alert for every word she spoke, the knock of her knife against the cutting board.

FINNEGAN HADN'T EXPECTED to see Chloe on New Year's Eve. He had stayed late at the restaurant to avoid the fact that he had nowhere to go, although he told himself that he was giving the kitchen a special cleaning for Lillian. But then, just as he was finishing, Chloe had come in with the red suitcase in her hand, and his sudden fear that she might be leaving loosened his tongue.

He hadn't really thought about what he was doing when he put the blue notebook in her suitcase. As much as anything, he just wanted to continue the feeling of New Year's Eve—at least the part until she'd dashed out the door. He knew it was a risk; he'd seen how prickly she could be when the produce delivery guy flirted with her, but he did it anyway and waited for the repercussions.

So, when he saw the notebook out on the counter one day when he came in to work, saw how full it was of words, his heart leapt. That night after work, he dug through the employee files to find her address, and the next Monday he went to her house, prepared for rebuff. But Isabelle had been there, all smiles and winks, practically shoving Chloe out the door. And the drive to the waterfall had been peaceful, easy, Chloe slowly softening over the hours. He had kept quiet, letting her relax, feeling her shed her protective layers.

He hadn't taken her to the waterfall in order to kiss her—somehow that seemed like the Northwest equivalent of inviting a girl to see your etchings. Nor was it his first kiss—there had been the time when the entire girls' gymnastics team decided that reaching his lips provided an acrobatic challenge sufficient for course credit. But when it happened, when the arch of the rocks and the wall of water pulled them together, he realized it was the first time he had felt truly happy since before his parents had left for Everest.

He should have known she'd change her mind, given even half a moment. Why would she want some altitudinous dishwasher? The silence of the ride home from the waterfall was utterly different than the trip south, the friendly rhythm of the windshield wipers turned into a steady refrain—you blew it, you blew it, you blew it. Chloe scrunched down in her seat and did a questionable impersonation of someone sleeping, while Finnegan drove, wishing as always, but for new and different reasons, that he could make himself smaller.

AND THAT WAS PRETTY MUCH how it stayed for months, Finnegan and Chloe playing an endless game of keep-away in the restaurant kitchen. In frustration, Finnegan took to the streets, running his way through the pair of shoes Aunt Ailis had packed in his car. He didn't care where he went as long as it was far enough to tire every muscle in his legs, steep enough to make his breath rip through his lungs. When he returned home, he would stand under the hot water in the shower until one of his roommates banged on the bathroom door. After he dressed, he would attack the apartment kitchen, tossing greasy takeout containers, working his way to the bottom of the sink.

He knew he should just give up, or go home or go on, depending. It seemed fairly obvious he wasn't going to get anywhere with Chloe. He had helped with Isabelle's ritual, thinking perhaps if Chloe saw him outside the restaurant, inside her house, it would change her attitude, but she seemed determined to ignore him. Still, he thought, anyone who was so intent on avoiding you had to be thinking about you an awful lot. It was an odd thing to hang your hope on, but it was what he had.

Spring gave way to summer. One morning on his run, he saw a small white-haired figure in purple tennis shoes up ahead. He ducked slightly as he ran by, hoping to pass without notice.

"Finnegan?"

Despite, or perhaps because of, her missing social filter, Aunt Ailis had always insisted he be polite. He stopped and turned.

"Hello, Isabelle."

"I thought it might be you."

"Hard to miss."

"Hard to hide?" She smiled. "Where have you been? You haven't come by the house since my ritual day."

"Yeah, well."

"Chloe doesn't know what she's doing—you know that, right?" Isabelle always did seem to get right to the point.

"She seems pretty certain to me."

"Yes, well. I think I was just as determined to have my husband as Chloe is not to have you. Women aren't always right."

Finnegan nodded, unconvinced.

"Do you feel like walking a bit?" Isabelle said. "I'd love some company."

It was the middle of his run, the point where fatigue was starting to hum in his muscles, shifting him from a mental being to a simply physical one, but he nodded again and let her set the pace. He wondered sometimes if anybody who wasn't his height could truly understand what it meant for him to pull in his stride, the way it cinched up his muscles, made every short step feel like he might lose his balance and fall. It hadn't felt that way with Chloe, which had seemed nothing short of miraculous to him.

Okay, Finnegan told himself, that was why he ran, to avoid thinking. He cast about for familiar territory.

"Tell me about your husband," he said to Isabelle. He could feel a story radiating from her; you could almost see them if you looked, especially in older people who had so many that they seemed to spill out like boxes from a loaded closet. It took only a simple question to open the door.

"We had a daughter," Isabelle said, "then another, and a son."

It was intriguing how people came at their stories, Finnegan thought as he listened to Isabelle. He had learned to watch the gap between question and answer, having realized that the less obvious the connection the more interesting the material left unsaid. Diving into the gap yourself was rarely productive, but if allowed to talk uninterrupted, the storyteller would eventually build bridges across it, bridges made of memories that felt safe and familiar, anecdotes that had turned solid and durable with the retelling. After a while, you could go fishing.

So Finnegan let Isabelle talk. He knew, from overhearing Chloe and Lillian in the kitchen, that Isabelle's son was relocating to the Northwest. For an archaeological dig on the Olympic Peninsula, he had said, but Chloe knew it was in order to live closer to his mother, and Finnegan could sense her relief that Isabelle would have family near her again. As Isabelle and Finnegan walked down the sidewalk, Isabelle told him happily about the family reunion at the cabin that Abby was planning, to mark the passing of the keys to Tom and Lillian. Even Isabelle's other daughter, Lucy, was coming, all the way from— Isabelle stopped, frustrated.

"Somewhere warm," she said. "Far away.

"Kangaroos," she added triumphantly.

When they reached Isabelle's house, she turned at the gate to face him.

"Would you like to talk again sometime?" she asked.

Finnegan glanced toward the house.

"It wouldn't have to be here. Coffee? You're so easy to talk to."

He knew when he was being handled, but old habits were hard to break.

"Sure," said Finnegan.

THE FIRST TIME, he simply listened, letting her stories wash over him. He could see that Isabelle's gaps were larger than most and not always created by ordinary emotional hesitation. She would approach the edge of a thought and the anecdotes and memories that would have carried her across years before now dissolved beneath her. While she could still find her way to the coffee shop where they met, he learned that standing in line behind her was not only polite but necessary if she was actually to get the coffee she wanted and not what she ordered, which might have unusual, if poetic, misfires in vocabulary—*latte, extra varnish; laughter, extra vacancies.*

On their second "date," as Isabelle liked to call them, he brought a blue notebook. He had tried to go without, had hoped he could make the transition into solely listening rather than recording, but the stories Isabelle still remembered were so brilliantly alive he couldn't resist.

"Chloe has a notebook like that," Isabelle said when he set it on the table.

He remembered his joy when he realized Chloe was writing in the notebook, the sadness he felt when it vanished along with any affection she appeared to have felt for him.

"She keeps it on her nightstand," Isabelle noted casually.

The third time they met, Isabelle sat down with her coffee—*latte, extra vanilla*—and smiled.

"Now," she said. "That's enough of me. Tell me why you write."

Maybe it was the blaring steam of the milk frother and the voices of the stroller-moms swirling around them, making him feel as if anything he said would be heard, at best, by Isabelle and perhaps not even then. Maybe it was—and he felt a twinge of contrition about this—the thought that Isabelle would likely forget his stories even before she left the coffee shop and thus they might almost never have been told. But Finnegan closed Isabelle's notebook and began to talk.

He told her about his parents and the big, clear skies of Boulder. The way the clouds of Portland had made him feel at first as if there was yet another barrier between himself and his mother and father, a direct route cut off by weather. He told her about being tall, the way the world could look so much smaller or larger from that height, depending on the day. He told her about Maridel and Hannah. Simon and Jasper and Viola. He told her about seeing Chloe at the vegetable stand, following her to the restaurant. New Year's Eve and all the months since. The way, even with all that, all the confusion about staying or going, the restaurant felt like home.

"That makes sense," Isabelle said.

"What?"

"You're a lot like her."

"Chloe?"

Isabelle shook her head. "Although that would make things interesting. I meant Lillian." She sipped her coffee, seeming to enjoy his puzzlement. "Food, stories. They aren't that different, you know. Speaking of which, I have a favor to ask."

"What?"

"Could I have that notebook?"

Finnegan was still trying to understand Isabelle's observations, but that was not particularly unusual. Sometimes what she said made sense later, and sometimes it didn't. In any event, this was her notebook, he told himself. She should have it if she wanted it.

But what if she forgot about it? What if she didn't pass it on to her children and the stories were lost? There was no getting them back once they were gone. They would scatter and no one would know where they were or who they had been.

Isabelle looked across the table at him, as if she could read every one of his thoughts even as her own became a mystery to her. She nodded calmly, waiting. Finnegan picked up the notebook and then, with a long exhalation, pushed it across the table to Isabelle.

THE DINNER CROWD was long gone, the restaurant closed. Finnegan was the last one in the kitchen. He enjoyed the solitude, the piano music he could put on the CD player without asking anyone else's opinion. It was easier, too, being here without Chloe, and he liked cleaning the nooks and crannies of the kitchen after everyone else was gone. Lillian was looking unbelievably pregnant these days and it gave him satisfaction to know he was giving her an easier start every morning when she arrived. He was grateful, not just for his job but for the atmosphere she created in her kitchen. Cleaning it was a way of saying thank you.

All his life, Finnegan had dealt with the freak-show

nature of his existence. The curiosity on everyone's faces that made him wish he could simply tattoo his long arms with answers to the inevitable questions: No, my parents weren't giants. No, I don't play basketball. No, I don't need an oxygen mask. But here in Lillian's kitchen he felt simply tall, one of a group of capable people who worked together. Lillian treated each person—dishwasher, cook, server, or customer—with the same respect she accorded the ingredients in her hands, and her attitude affected the entire staff.

He smiled as he wiped down the faucet of the dish sink, the last thing he always did before going home.

The kitchen door opened with a bang.

"You're such an idiot!" Finnegan heard a voice behind him.

He cautiously straightened, turned. Chloe.

"The notebooks," she said. And then she walked across the kitchen and kissed him.

Finnegan had no idea what she was talking about, but he decided that this was one question he was not required to ask. He simply lifted her up to the counter so that what was happening could continue as long as possible without wrecking his back.

Chloe's cell phone rang. She pulled away from Finnegan and reached into her pocket.

"Seriously?" Finnegan said. This couldn't happen twice. If she started to run, he'd just stick her in the dish sink. It was pretty big; she would fit. She'd never stay there, but at least it would slow her down.

"It might be Isabelle," Chloe said, shaking her head at him. She glanced at the caller ID.

"It's Tom." She looked concerned and clicked the answer button.

Finnegan watched as Chloe listened. He could hear the rumble of Tom's voice on the other end of the line, excitement running through the cadence of the sentences.

Finnegan raised his eyebrows quizzically. Chloe grinned and mouthed one word—*baby.*

The

LOVE SEAT

It was late September, and Al sat at his usual table in Lillian's restaurant, eating Cajun chicken gumbo for lunch. It was funny, he thought, not for the first time and not with any particular humor, how being alone meant one thing when you were on a break from your marriage, and quite another when your marriage had taken a break from you.

"How's it going?" Chloe had come out of the kitchen and was standing next to his table. She looked happier these days, Al thought. He had seen her walking down the street the other night with Finnegan, laughter bouncing back and forth between them. And honestly, her gumbo was inspired.

"It's great," Al replied.

"You're not happy." Chloe observed him, head cocked to one side.

"It's wonderful," he said. "Just the right spices."

"Not the soup," she said.

The front door opened and Lillian entered, carrying a baby. The dining room rippled with pleased noises; Lillian smiled and made her way toward Al and Chloe, stopping occasionally to say hello to her customers and let them greet the baby inside the blanket.

"How's everything over here?" she asked as she arrived at Al's table.

"Al's not happy," Chloe said.

"I'm fine," Al said, shifting his chair so he could see Lillian better. "How's Clementine?"

Lillian leaned down so Al could see the baby's face. "Just great," Lillian said.

"She's beautiful," he commented, resisting the urge to reach out and touch the baby's cheek. "And bigger than a week ago. How much weight has she gained?"

"Quit deflecting, Al." Chloe turned to Lillian. "It's been six months since Louise left; he needs to do something."

Lillian nodded in agreement, shifting Clementine so she could watch the conversation. The baby's eyes gazed at Al, big and dark and full of inquiry.

"How about a ritual?" Chloe asked.

"I don't have the book anymore," Al said to the baby. "Louise took it."

. . .

IT WAS CHLOE who had given Al a ride home the night of Isabelle's party in March. She had caught him as he was leaving on foot.

"Do you want a ride?" she asked.

"It's not far, I can walk."

"Well, I'm taking you, anyway," Chloe said. "I owe you one—that's the happiest I've seen Isabelle in a long time."

Chloe's car seemed held together with duct tape and wire, but Al—who washed his car once a week for the sheer pleasure of watching the steel-blue color come up through the suds—understood her affection for her vehicle. The ride to his house had been quiet, Chloe and Al both contentedly tired from their efforts of the day. Al was particularly pleased by the success of Isabelle's throne. He had enjoyed working on it with Finnegan; the young man's fingers held a magical creativity, and the designs that flowed onto the wooden surface of the chair had often made Al blink with surprise.

He started to mention it to Chloe, only to be cut off by a scream of brakes in the distance. Chloe jerked her own car to a stop and they both strained forward, listening, but there was no sound of impact. The night returned to a deep quiet; they relaxed and smiled at each other, and Chloe continued driving.

"Sounded like a close call," she said.

"People are driving too fast these days," Al remarked. "Louise told me she almost got hit the other day.

"I'm halfway down this next block on the right," he added.

His house was completely dark, Al realized as they approached, a black hole in an otherwise welcoming string of lights illuminating front porches and bedroom or living room windows. From the glow of the streetlamp, Al could see his car was missing. Perhaps Louise had gone to the grocery store; she had mentioned something that morning about being out of milk. But even if Louise had gone out, she would have left lights on. She didn't like coming back to darkness, even when she was just going from room to room. Al generally tried not to say anything, even as he mentally calculated the cost to the environment and their utility bill. It was no wonder the bulbs were always burning out.

"That's odd," he said, looking at the house.

"I'll come in with you, just to make sure everything's all right." Chloe was still thinking about the almost-accident, he could tell. She had driven with extra care those last few blocks.

Al made his way cautiously up the driveway and then went instinctively to the side door—Louise liked keeping the front entry clean of everyday dirt. The small porch was darkness itself and Al had to feel for the edge of each of the steps, holding on to the railing. As he reached the top, his foot landed on something brittle; it broke with a quick snap and then crunch. Behind him, Chloe pulled out her phone and the light of the screen illuminated bits of glass on the porch.

Al avoided horror movies, but he knew that this was how the bad parts started, the small sound in the dark, the minor detail out of place. He stood, listening for any noise that would give him direction. He imagined Louise, sprawled across their bed, blood dripping from her slit throat. Or taken, stuffed in his trunk and left somewhere.

Al took a breath and put his hand on the doorknob; it wasn't locked. He took a cautious step inside the kitchen and turned on the switch. Nothing happened. He reached for the flashlight Louise kept in the cabinet by the door and swept its beam across the kitchen. He could see glass covering the floor, broken curves catching the light, filaments glittering like mica in sand. But otherwise, strangely, everything was in place, except a chair pulled up against the counter. It didn't make any sense.

The beam caught on a note lying on the table. It had his name on it—Louise's handwriting, but rushed, full of adrenaline. Did they make victims write their own ransom notes? Trying to steady his breathing, Al picked it up and opened it.

Two words: Buy Lightbulbs.

Chloe was watching Al's face.

"Should we call someone?" she asked.

Al shook his head; there was no one you could call for something like this.

IT HAD TAKEN HOURS to clean up all the glass, although Al had noted at one point that most of it was contained in the kitchen, for which he was oddly grateful. Chloe had gone to the store and returned with two pairs of rubber gloves and a bag full of lightbulbs, which they put in, one per room at first, like a chain of small campfires throughout the otherwise pitch-black house.

Chloe never asked any questions, which was a good thing, as Al was pretty sure he didn't have answers. Louise was gone, that was clear. The fact that she wasn't coming back took a little longer to reveal itself.

In those first weeks, he had thought about hiring a private detective, but the note on the table always stopped him. That, and the fact that she had taken his car and the book of rituals. He could understand why she would want to leave him; couldn't fault her, really, for that. But the car, the book. Those rankled.

Still, he didn't know what to do, exactly. It had been six months now since Louise had left and he still walked about the muted colors of a house that had never felt like his, unsure each time he came home and opened the door if she would be there or not. There had been no activity on her cell phone or credit card, after the charge that night at a gas station near the Oregon border. Which seemed to be an answer in itself. Still, Louise liked to complete things, come full circle—although whether that had already happened or was yet to come, Al wasn't certain. And without certainty, his life hung, motionless.

"What do *you* want?" Finnegan had asked him recently. "You don't have to wait to see what she does." Implied in the statement was their shared understanding that the waiting had no particular end-point.

And now, here were Lillian and Chloe, standing by his table at the restaurant, asking him to make that point definitive.

"You don't need the book to tell you what to do," Lillian said, dipping down to kiss the top of her baby's head. "Think about the best thing she did, and the worst. And then let go."

SEPTEMBER WAS A BUSY TIME of year for accountants, and not particularly Al's favorite. All the corporations that had filed extensions in April had to have their taxes in by the middle of September, with the procrastinating individuals following close behind. Al's clients who hadn't been able to get their finances together in the spring were even less inclined to now, any more than they wanted to tuck in the loose ends of their carefree summer spending—the boat and bicycle rentals, the mai tais and Manhattans that matched the colors of the slowly fading sunsets of August. In September, accountants were firmly planted in the role of curmudgeon, grown-up, when everyone wanted only to remember the feeling of bare feet for as long as possible. So Al was glad to shut the door of his office and start his walk home.

Al had fixed Louise's taillight after she left, but in the end, he never felt comfortable using her car. Chloe told him he should sell the car and buy something for himself, as it seemed less and less likely that he would see his old Cadillac again. Most days, however, it seemed simpler just to walk, and Al found he liked the time it gave him between work and home, a chance to let go of the day and get ready for the empty house ahead of him. Sometimes he'd stop by Isabelle's on the way for a glass of wine, and end up cooking dinner with her while Chloe was at the restaurant. It was easy being with Isabelle, who didn't ask a lot of probing questions, even when they'd figured out that it was his Louise who had brought Isabelle her coat.

"She was a pilot," Isabelle had commented.

Al shook his head, puzzled.

"Well, in any case, she flew."

And with that, Al couldn't argue.

But after Chloe and Lillian's little intervention at the restaurant that day, Al didn't feel like talking to anybody, even Isabelle. As he walked up his driveway, he kept his attention studiously on the house. For the past ten years, they'd had a gardener, but after Louise left, Al forgot to pay him so many times the man simply stopped coming. Now the grass was well past ankle height.

"Excuse me," said a voice behind him. Al turned and saw his neighbor from a few houses down. Nancy spent almost all her time in her yard, a constantly changing array of relentlessly cheery annuals—marigolds and geraniums and impatiens. As she was the only other woman on the block without children or grandchildren, Al had once thought she might be a good friend for Louise, but Louise had wanted nothing to do with her.

"Al," said Nancy. "It is Al, isn't it?"

As if he didn't pass her house every day, commenting politely each time the color palette changed.

"Yes."

"Well, Al . . ." She looked uncomfortable. "I mean. Well. The lawn."

Al looked down the block to Nancy's house, where the lawn was, as always, trim and smooth as her own well-exercised figure.

"No, Al. Yours."

"Oh."

"I mean. I think we'd all appreciate it if . . . Well, you know."

"Yes." He supposed he did.

"Good, then!" Nancy smiled happily. "I'm sure it'll make you feel better, too."

Al watched her walk back down the sidewalk. The quick little strides, the sprightly assurance of her shoulders. He shook his head and looked about him. His grass sprawled out before him, shaggy and rough-edged, the Mickey Rourke of lawns.

"Well, okay," he said. It hadn't rained in a couple of days, although it was due to soon. It might be his last chance for a while.

He opened the garage and dug through the boxes to the back, where he found his old gas lawn mower. He went upstairs and changed from his work clothes into a pair of jeans, as beat-up as the lawn, and a gray T-shirt, proclaiming allegiance to a college he hadn't seen in thirty years. He was surprised to find both pants and shirt to be a bit baggier than he remembered. It must have been all the walking, he decided, as he took a quick look in the mirror to make sure.

The lawn mower waited on the front lawn where he had left it, its once bright red paint dulled by dust to something closer to pink. Al leaned over and grasped the starter handle and yanked up, feeling the cord unwind within the machine, the sound of the engine almost catching.

It took ten increasingly sweaty tries, but finally the motor roared into life, throwing gas fumes into the air, bringing with them a heady mix of nostalgia and swagger. Al aimed the mower toward the opposite end of the yard, feeling the vibrations of the engine through his outstretched arms, the pressure against the balls of his feet as he pushed off, one step after another, bits of grass spewing out the side of the machine and into the catcher, the smell thick and green in the air.

Think about the best thing Louise ever did, Lillian had said. As Al pushed the mower, he considered the challenge. He had to get past the gaping hole that was Louise's departure, but the lawn mower was patient—moving back and forth, back and forth, leaving a long, clean aisle of cut grass behind him. His thoughts wandered, released by the actions of his muscles.

And then he remembered—his wedding, after the ceremony, at the reception. He had been talking to his father, when he saw his mother across the room. She'd left her second husband by that point—he was as boring as Al had always thought, apparently—and she had come to the wedding alone. She looked so uncertain standing by herself, but Al couldn't get away from the conversation he was in. And then Louise walked up to his mother and asked her to dance.

Al remembered the way the other guests stared at the two women out on the dance floor, but what he remembered more was the smile on his mother's face. He hadn't thought about that in a long time. Funny, how he could recall his mother's expression better than he could remember the woman his wife had been.

There was a time, in the beginning of their marriage, when he and Louise told each other their thoughts. Over dinner, Louise would listen, fascinated by the tales of love and deception and sacrifice he gleaned from his clients' financial information. He ignored any qualms about confidentiality, returning from his day at the office bearing stories like a hunter-gatherer, until somewhere along the line it all changed and the only plot point Louise cared about was whether or not the client had paid his invoice.

But in the beginning, Al thought, they had been different. "Had been" being, as Louise had taught him when they were in college, the past-perfect verb tense—a grammatical form you didn't want to linger in too long, as it made a paragraph cumbersome. Besides, Al thought, as a name, the term was usually only half correct.

Once, a few years back, Al had suggested to Louise that they take one of Lillian's cooking classes. He thought about it for a long time before saying anything, worried that her presence in the restaurant might ruin what had become an increasingly important part of his life, but the selfishness of that was too obvious and he asked her, hoping that some of the magic he felt might rub off onto his marriage. What would happen to Louise, he wondered, if she was given the first bite of Lillian's homemade cantaloupe ice cream, or was encouraged to make her own salad dressing from scratch, no necessary ingredients, no right or wrong.

"Don't you like what I cook?" Louise asked, clearly offended, and Al had dropped the subject with a mingled sense of relief and regret.

Somewhere along the line, theirs had become a

marriage of covert agents, all the real communication in code. Al knew by the color of the nightgown his wife wore to bed what his chances were of getting lucky that night. If he saw his place at the dinner table set with a fork but no napkin, his mind would search back through the day to find where he had offended; if his laundry was folded in sharp creases, he understood the explanation was coming soon; if it was left in the basket, it would take a few days longer.

Some days, Louise would call at the office and ask him to pick up milk, or stamps, or toothpaste, any of the items two blocks out of her way on errands she was going to do anyway. He knew what she actually wanted—his clients often did the same thing, asking him for information they could easily find on the Internet or in documentation he had already supplied. Their calls almost always came after the receipt of an invoice, or when their tax estimate was higher than anticipated. A need for service, a balancing of life's perceived inequities. He responded to his clients—he wouldn't last long in his business if he didn't—but after a while, when it came to Louise, a certain obstinacy rose up in him.

He could see that it would do him no good simply to refuse her requests, or to point out the illogical nature of them. So he would claim to have forgotten when she asked, blaming the busyness of his day, his general lack of memory, hiding under a cloak of befuddlement. Every fourth request, or fifth, when he could feel the balance between his sense of self and her disdain shifting into a danger zone, he did the task she required and the scales recalibrated, a little less even each time.

The irony was that he actually enjoyed going to the grocery store, the feeling of a cold half-gallon of milk in his hands; when Louise had been out of town visiting her mother, he had gone shopping for food every day after work, just for the fun of walking down the aisles and choosing between the selections. What grated on him about Louise's requests was how minor they were, the very smallness of them just another way of telling him he was unnecessary, as if everything else he did during the day was worth nothing if this was all he could be trusted to do.

And that was it, he realized. That was the worst thing.

The mower caught on a stick in the grass and it snapped, shooting out pieces to either side. Al jumped back, and then looked, almost equally surprised, at the lawn in front of him. The lines rolled out, neat and even. The job was done.

Not without effort, however. Al could feel the sweat running down the back of his shirt. He returned the lawn mower to the garage and went upstairs to take a shower. In his bedroom, he passed his dresser and saw Louise's note. He had placed it there the night she left and somehow never moved it; he saw it every morning when he got up and every night before he went to bed. In an odd way, he realized now, it was a bit like having a wife.

Al paused, looked in the direction of the shower, and then picked up the note, stuck it in his back pocket, and went downstairs. In the kitchen, he poured himself a large glass of red wine and walked into the beige-carpeted living room, where food and beverages were strictly prohibited. As he approached the love seat, his toe caught on the edge of the coffee table and the wine slopped over the rim of the glass and down onto the creamy-white fabric.

He stopped, horrified. He turned his head to the right, to the left, listening. Silence.

Al stared at the love seat for a long moment. Its sleek arms that would never be wide enough to hold a glass, the slightly curved back that seemed to promise a soft landing but never did. The sweet little wooden feet that always snagged his toes if the coffee table hadn't done it first. With a small shrug, he took his wineglass and tilted it, spilling its dark red contents in a long, sinuous line down the length of the cushions.

It was a deeply unattractive stain; someone who didn't know better might suspect a murder and start looking for dead bodies. Al went to the far end of the love seat and shoved, using the same muscles he had just employed with the lawn mower, pushing the love seat across the carpet and then down the wooden hallway, leaving thin white scratches behind him in the cherry flooring. When he got to the front door, he grabbed the base of one end and hoisted it skyward. It just fit in the frame of the door.

Louise had been right that it was the correct size for their house, after all.

Al jammed his shoulder against the underside of the love seat, propelling it forward along its curved back and down the porch stairs. It landed vertical again at the bottom. Another shove and the process was repeated, down the walk, end over end, the love seat picking up speed like a hay bale until it reached the curb, where its trajectory ended with a final, ignominious thump.

Al stood back, considering the scene in front of him with satisfaction. The love seat was a bit worse for wear; there was a line of dirt running along the top, and one of the wooden feet sported a white patch of paint where it had scraped against the door frame. He kind of liked it.

He positioned the love seat on the parking strip facing the street. Then he went back into the house, got a new glass of red wine, and returned, flopping down on the seat. He sat, still breathing a bit heavily, sweat dripping down his temples, through his shirt and onto the fabric of the couch, the euphoria of destruction simmering in his veins. He could feel years of anger leaving his body one tired muscle at a time. It was wonderful. He leaned back, throwing his arm over the top of the love seat, and the note crinkled in his pocket.

Louise's note—his paper wife. He thought of the real Louise, smashing her way through their house. The anger she must have had to do that. Funny, how after all those years, this was what they finally had in common. He took a long sip of wine.

Al knew that most people assumed the end of his marriage happened the night of Isabelle's party. But sitting there on the love seat, he realized that it probably began ending right at the beginning—that day in the cafeteria when he first met Louise. He had seen a girl with a sandwich in her hand and fallen in love with the part of her that made sense to him, that fit the particular story he knew how to read. That was the woman he had lived with for over thirty years.

But the woman who could smash lightbulbs? He hadn't known she existed—and yet he understood now that she must have been there all the time, hidden by the blinkers of his own vision. He had seen the bite out of the sandwich and missed the elbows on the table. It was, perhaps, as simple and complicated as that. It made him ponder what she had missed about him—what, in fact, he might have missed about himself.

Down the street, he saw a figure approaching, a man in jeans and a sweatshirt, with one of those lumpy marsupial carriers they used to transport babies these days. Tom, Al realized. He worried for a moment what Tom might think about the whole love-seat-on-the-curb thing, but when Al saw Tom's face, he could tell the only thing the man was thinking about was sleep.

"Al," Tom said, as he approached.

"How are you doing?"

"She likes to be walked," Tom replied, sitting down next to Al, oblivious to the stain on the seat, careful only not to wake the sleeping baby. "Lillian asked me to give her a go around the block. And then Clem here fell asleep so we just kept going."

Al handed Tom his glass of wine.

"Nice," Tom said. He drained it slowly and gratefully.

"How's fatherhood?"

"I've never been so tired. But, you know . . ." He paused and looked down at the baby, love falling across his face.

Al nodded, even though he knew he didn't.

"You know," Tom said after a moment, glancing sideways at Al, "I mean, it's a lot to ask, but we could really use some help."

"I think we just might need some more wine," Al said quickly, and headed to the kitchen, hiding his grin.

He came back with the bottle and a second glass, and the two men sat side by side on the love seat, gazing out at the neighborhood, listening to the baby snuffle in her sleep. After a while, Nancy drove down the street in her gray Passat station wagon; as she passed, she slowed the car and waved, a bit uncertainly. Al and Tom raised their glasses, over the head of the sleeping baby.

EPILOGUE

Louise walked down the main street of the tiny coastal town. Calling it "main" was probably an overstatement, she thought, as there was really only one street, leading from the narrow highway to the ocean itself. The roads that branched off, a block or two at most, held the houses of the few year-round residents and the summer cottages of the more affluent. A quiet place, generally. It had felt like home the minute she turned off the highway five months ago, Al's blue Cadillac sputtering into a prima donna refusal to go one more mile after the seven-hour drive down I-5, across the valleys of Oregon to the coast.

She had wanted to reach the ocean. She'd heard that the coastline was jagged and windswept, with rogue waves that could reach out of the ocean and grab an unsuspecting sightseer. What she found was a small town with a string of brown-shingled buildings, none of them substantial, and yet, strung together like that, they somehow felt solid, ready to hold out against waves of water or weather or tourists.

The car had died at five-thirty on that Saturday morning back in March, bucking to a stop in front of the only lit commercial building in town—Joe's Bakery. According to Joe, who sat her on a stool and gave her coffee and warm bread even though he wasn't open yet, the closest mechanic was fifty miles away but, more to the point, was still on his winter sojourn in Mexico and wouldn't be back for two weeks. Towing the car was impossible in any case; when she got out her AAA card, she realized it was expired, which was when she remembered putting the renewal notice on the top of Al's to-do pile a few months back. And of course, no one was going to believe that she had suddenly become inspired to pay her AAA invoice at the crack of dawn on a Saturday, only to call back later with a story about amazing coincidences. So that was that. She had grabbed money when she left, but not enough to cover a big tow job and still have any left to—to what? she wondered. Have a vacation? Start a life? What was she doing, anyway?

Louise looked down and was surprised to see the piece of bread that Joe had given her was already gone. Joe looked over and grinned. He was a wiry man, probably sixty years old, with forearms solid as tree branches and a dusting of white hair across the top of his head.

"Want another slice?" he asked. She nodded. The last thing she'd eaten was the apple she'd brought along when she went to stake out Isabelle's house. While she was driving, she hadn't thought of being hungry, her mind so loud she couldn't hear her stomach. But now, she was starving.

"So, what are you going to do?" Joe asked.

What she was going to do, apparently, was get a job working the lunch shift at Joe's pizza parlor next door. The kid he had hired in preparation for the summer tourist season had figured out that the surf was better and warmer in California. Joe didn't care that Louise's pizza experience was nonexistent. That afternoon, he set her up at the industrial dough machine, adding in flour and water as the mixing blade revolved around a bowl big enough that Louise could have put a beach's worth of sand in it. He taught her how to crank open the giant cans of whole tomatoes and then crush them, adding roasted garlic and oregano. How to use the back of a soup ladle to spread the thick red sauce across the smooth surface of the dough, following it with handfuls of grated cheese and all the toppings the customers could think of. She learned the quick thrust and jerk with the wooden peel, sliding the pizza onto the hot floor of the wood-fired oven. It felt good.

During the next few months, she got her first oven

burn. A small rental house. An air-dry haircut. And, in the last stretch of calm before the tourists descended, the best sex of her life, back in the prep area of the kitchen, with Joe, who, as she might have guessed, had very good hands.

As time went on, she wondered sometimes about Al. She wondered if he had fixed the taillight on her car, if he'd gotten a house-cleaner. She was surprised at how little she missed him, and how rarely he entered her thoughts. She wondered if it had always been like that or had only become so over time. If somehow she could have changed the balance, if she, or they, had tried.

But in the end, she had no desire to find out. Every evening after work, she would walk out of the pizza parlor and hear the waves landing on the beach nearby. She'd go home and take a shower, and then, hair still wet, gin and tonic in hand, she would wander out onto the sand and watch the sun moving slowly toward the end of its day, lighting the people who strolled along the beach. At first, their arms would be at their sides or clutched across their chests, protection against the cooling air, but as they made their way down the endless expanse of the beach, they would slowly but surely raise them until it almost looked as if they were flying.

BY OCTOBER, the summer residents had gone, reassembling their city selves even as they packed their cars, remembering their need for brand-labeled cappuccinos and dry cleaners and dinner reservations, relegating to nostalgia the joy of a slice of sloppy pizza, the feeling of suntanned skin letting off the heat of the day, warming the sheets at night.

Louise walked down the quiet street, on her break between making dough and chopping pizza toppings. It was her fifty-second birthday, but she couldn't complain about her age to Joe, who would just laugh and call her a spring chicken. It was her birthday, though, and she decided she deserved a present, so she stopped in the bookstore. Amy, who owned it, had called to tell her that the Agatha Christie novel she asked about had come in.

The bookstore was small and elegant, its books carefully chosen to appeal to both the casual tourist and those who stayed through the long and stormy winters. A mix of bright and subtle covers, rough-edged pages and slippery paperbacks. A flurry of handwritten notes hung from the bottom of the shelves, offering recommendations and brief synopses, inviting hands to open the books above.

When Louise entered the store, Amy was already helping another customer, so Louise wandered off to look at the books. While she was browsing, a somewhat portly man with curling white hair and a black fedora entered the store and made his way to the front desk. He said something to Amy, who nodded with delight and retrieved a small stack of two books. The man took out a pen and started to write on the title page of each book, the other customer watching with barely contained excitement.

After the man and the other customer left, Louise walked over. Amy reached under the counter to take the Agatha Christie novel from its holding place.

"Here's your book," she said. "I can't believe there's one of hers you haven't read."

Louise got out her wallet to pay.

"No way," Amy said. "It's your birthday."

"How did you know?"

"Joe. Remember, you filled out an application to work for him. We all know your age now."

"Who was that guy, by the way?" Louise asked, deflecting the amusement in Amy's eyes. "The one with the fedora?"

"Oh—that was an author."

"Do you know him?"

"No, I've never seen him before; he just walked in and offered to autograph his books. Kind of thrilling, isn't it?"

AGATHA CHRISTIE NOVEL in hand, Louise headed in the direction of her rental house. She could see the beach at the end of the street, knew before her feet ever touched the sand the way it would stretch out in front of her, the sky a great, wide arc reaching down to touch the water. She swung her arms as she walked, feeling the weight of the book shift forward and back. She thought about the man she had seen in the store, the way Amy and the other customer had watched him as he signed the books. No one had ever asked him for identification, Louise realized.

The author could have been anyone, really.

"Huh," Louise said, and smiled.

Acknowledgments

A book is born of many mothers, female and male, and raised by even more. This one would not have existed without some serendipitous encounters and the help of many supportive people.

It was Laura Esquivel who told me about celebrating fifty-second birthdays in Mexico, which got me thinking about the power of ritual and the need to occasionally toss a few plates. Melissa Gayle West, over a hot cup of coffee, taught me the whys and hows of celebration and remembrance. Don Busch served as my resident expert in all things tax-related, while Rylan Bauermeister graciously shared his enthusiasm for numbers and rock climbing. Nancy Carroll related the story of Dorothy and Phyllis, a variation of which made its way into Maridel's character, a blue notebook of my own. Nina Meierding took me to Silver Falls, while the experience of attempting to move some furniture by myself taught me that you really can roll a love seat.

Words need ears to hear them and eyes to read them, long before they can ever be considered a book. Jennie Shortridge and Randy Sue Coburn have been along for the entire ride, reading every sentence, caring about each character. A bow of gratitude as well to my steadfast readers Genevieve Gagne-Hawes, Nina and Bill Meierding, Deedee Rechtin, Caitlin and Gloria Bauermeister, Neil Flagg, Sally Debono, Lisa Cooke, and my wonderful husband, Ben Bauermeister, who not only reads but graciously deals with fictional people taking over his life and kitchen on a regular basis.

There were the places of refuge, too, offered by the patron saints of writing. This book took some remarkable turns during two stays at Hedgebrook on Whidbey Island. And a special thank-you to Richard and Becca Niday at the Majestic Mountain Retreat in Rhododendron, Oregon, who have been so generous with their cabin; and to Jan Huston, who let me hide away in her guest cottage and listen to the frogs.

Then there are those who guide the words from me to you—my brilliant agent, Amy Berkower, and editors—Rachel Kahan, Sara Minnich, and Ivan Held; Katie McKee and Kate Stark, who know how to make a book feel like a party; the terrific sales force at Putnam and Berkley; and last but never least, the booksellers who do the hard and thoughtful work of knowing what you like and getting the books in your hands. May we always celebrate the community that is reading.

Readers Guide for

THE LOST ART OF MIXING

by Erica Bauermeister

Discussion Questions

1. At the beginning of the book, there is a quote by Aesop: "Every truth has two sides." What do you think is the importance of that quote to the novel as a whole?

2. At first glance, Al appears to be a staid accountant, comfortable with numbers and order, never doing anything unexpected. And yet he engages in a secretive and odd behavior: masquerading as a published author at nearby bookstores. Why does he do this? Did you find this strange or understandable?

3. Consider the relationships between Isabelle, her children Abby and Rory, and her grandson, Rory.

How do their familial ties differ from relationships that are based on friendship or love, such as Isabelle's bond with Chloe or Lillian?

4. In her family, Abby is regarded as the responsible one, a wet blanket who focuses on obligations instead of fun. Is this characterization fair? How does Abby see herself? What stereotypes or roles have been assigned to you that aren't entirely accurate?

5. Chloe and Finnegan's relationship is rife with false starts, progress forward, and then backward slides. What about their individual personalities prevents them from connecting at first?

6. Each chapter takes you deep into the perspective of a different character. How did this structure influence your views of the characters? Did your feelings about any of the protagonists change when you entered his or her point of view?

7. Think about the various rituals that take place in the novel—for instance, Chloe's walk with the empty suitcase, or Isabelle's birthday celebration. What is the importance of these rituals? What rituals do you practice in your own life, and what meaning do they hold for you?

8. What role do Finnegan's blue notebooks play in his life? What do you think it means to him when he hands Isabelle her book to keep?

9. Tom's character is struggling with a great loss, and his lingering sadness in many ways impedes his new relationship with Lillian. How did you feel about his emotional journey? What allowed him finally to move on?

10. In the novel, as in real life, a deeper issue often underlies a superficial conflict. What do lightbulbs mean to Louise? And to Al?

11. The author has referred to *The Lost Art of Mixing* as a series of dominoes, each character tipping another (or others) forward, often unknowingly. How does Louise and Abby's near miss at the intersection factor into the lives of the other characters? What might this say about life in general?

12. Which was your favorite character in the book, and why? Who did you relate to the most?

Keep reading
for an excerpt from

THE SCHOOL OF ESSENTIAL INGREDIENTS

by Erica Bauermeister

Now available
from Berkley Books

Lillian loved best the moment before she turned on the lights. She would stand in the restaurant kitchen doorway, rain-soaked air behind her, and let the smells come to her—ripe sourdough yeast, sweet-dirt coffee, and garlic, mellowing as it lingered. Under them, more elusive, stirred the faint essence of fresh meat, raw tomatoes, cantaloupe, water on lettuce. Lillian breathed in, feeling the smells move about and through her, even as she searched out those that might suggest a rotting orange at the bottom of a pile, or whether the new assistant chef was still double-dosing the curry dishes. She was. The girl was a daughter of a friend and good enough with knives, but some days, Lillian thought with a sigh, it was like trying to teach subtlety to a thunderstorm.

But tonight was Monday. No assistant chefs, no customers looking for solace or celebration. Tonight was Monday, cooking-class night.

After seven years of teaching, Lillian knew how her students would arrive on the first night of class—walking through the kitchen door alone or in ad hoc groups of two or three that had met up on the walkway to the mostly darkened restaurant, holding the low, nervous conversations of strangers who will soon touch one another's food. Once inside, some would clump together, making those first motions toward connection, while others would roam the kitchen, fingers stroking brass pots or picking up a glowing red pepper, like small children drawn to the low-hanging ornaments on a Christmas tree.

Lillian loved to watch her students at this moment—they were elements that would become more complex and intriguing as they mixed with one another, but at the beginning, placed in relief by their unfamiliar surroundings, their essence was clear. A young man reaching out to touch the shoulder of the still younger woman next to him—"What's your name?"—as her hand dropped to the stainless-steel counter and traced its smooth surface. Another woman standing alone, her mind still lingering with—a child? A lover? Every once in a while there was a couple, in love or ruins.

Lillian's students arrived with a variety of motivations, some drawn by a yearning as yet unmet to hear murmured culinary compliments, others who had come to find a cook rather than become one. A few participants had no desire for lessons at all, arriving with gift certificates in hand as if on a forced march to certain failure; they knew their cakes would always be flat, their cream sauces filled with small, disconcerting pockets of flour, like bills in your mailbox when you had hoped for a love letter.

And then there were those students who seemingly had no choice, who could no more stay out of a kitchen than a kleptomaniac could keep her hands in her pockets. They came early, stayed late, fantasized about leaving their corporate jobs and becoming chefs with an exhilarating mixture of guilt and pleasure. If Lillian's soul sought out this last group, it was only to be expected, but in truth, she found them all fascinating. Lillian knew that whatever their reasons for coming, at some moment in the course of the class each one's eyes would widen with joy or tears or resolution—it always happened. The timing and the reason would be different for each, and that's where the fascination lay. No two spices work the same.

The kitchen was ready. The long stainless-steel counters lay before her, expansive and cool in the dark. Lillian knew without looking that Robert had received the vegetable order from the produce man who delivered only on Mondays. Caroline would have stood over skinny, smart-mouthed Daniel until the floors were scrubbed, the thick rubber mats rinsed with the hose outside until they were black and shining. Beyond the swinging door on the other side of the kitchen, the dining room stood ready, a quiet field of tables under starched white linen, napkins folded into sharp triangles at each place. But no one would use the dining room tonight. All that mattered was the kitchen.

Lillian stretched her fingers once, twice, and turned on the light.

Keep reading
for an excerpt from

JOY FOR BEGINNERS

by Erica Bauermeister

Now available
from Berkley Books

Life came back slowly, Kate realized. It didn't come flooding in with the reassurance that all was well. The light outside was no different; her daughter's body, the strength of her hug, was not necessarily more substantial. The delicate veil Kate had placed between herself and the world was not flung away. It clung.

But life is persistent, slipping into your consciousness sideways, catching you with a fleeting moment of color, the unexpected and comforting smell of a neighbor's dinner cooking as you walk on a winter evening, the feeling of warm water running between your fingers as you wash the dishes at night. There is nothing so seductive as reality.

. . .

THE WOMEN WERE DUE to arrive soon; it was quiet in the house, and Kate was glad of the impending company. She was still not used to being alone with her body. For the past eighteen months it had been the property of others—doctors certainly, but also friends, relatives, her daughter—its boundaries and capacities something they measured, gambled on, watched with loving or terrified or clinical eyes. Now the medical professionals had declared it hers again, handing it back like an overdue and slightly scuffed library book. In the weeks between the doctor's appointment and her daughter's departure for college, Kate had filled the space around them with lists and plans, shopping trips for desk lamps and extra-long twin sheets for Robin's freshman dorm room. Now Robin was off and away and Kate felt sometimes as if she was living in two empty houses, one inside the other.

So it was nice to have the prospect of guests, even if they were hell-bent on jubilation. Kate had heard the excitement in her friends' voices when she invited them to dinner, a thank-you for all they had done for her, she explained. But Marion had quickly renamed the evening a victory party and insisted that it be a potluck.

"You wouldn't take the fun out of it for us, would you?" Marion had asked.

As Kate moved about the kitchen from stove to refrigerator to sink, she passed the bulletin board that served as a central hub for reminders and memories, its surface a collage of photographs, a calendar, old ticket stubs and coupons and take-out menus. The week before Robin had left for college, she had surreptitiously added a brochure. Kate had spotted it in the morning when she came into the kitchen to make coffee—the glossy photograph leaping out at her, an extravagantly yellow raft vaulting through churning brown waves, water drops flying off its sides in rainbows. Kate's friend Hadley, who had once worked in marketing, always called those photos "adventure porn."

When Robin had come through the kitchen, Kate pointed to the brochure with a raised eyebrow.

"They've got two openings for next summer," Robin said. "Wouldn't it be fantastic?"

Kate had looked at her daughter's eyes, so full of anticipation and, deep underneath, a plea for normalcy. They had spent too much of the past year in a world full of exit doors, Kate thought. They could both use a promise that they would be here a year from now.

How could you say no? And yet as Kate had looked at the raft, the water, the size of it all, that had been exactly what—in fact the only thing—she wanted to say.

THE DOORBELL RANG, ten minutes early. Caroline, guessed Kate with an inward smile, as she opened the door.

"I thought you might want some help," Caroline said

as she entered, arms overflowing with a wooden salad bowl and a bottle of champagne. She put them down on the small table by the front door and gave Kate a quick, fierce hug.

"What needs doing?" she asked, as she headed toward the kitchen.

Kate followed her and gestured to the wrought iron table on the back patio. Caroline walked over to the silverware drawer, sidestepping around Kate, who had opened the refrigerator to get out the sour cream.

"Cloth napkins?" Caroline asked, a fistful of forks in her right hand.

"The green ones in the sideboard."

"How's the house without Robin?" Caroline called as she rummaged through the drawer in the dining room, pulling out seven napkins.

"Quiet. And yours?"

"Empty." Caroline laughed softly. "We're quite the pair, aren't we?"

The kitchen was quiet for a few minutes. Kate could hear the soft clink of forks against knives as Caroline set the table outside. Kate lifted the foil on the pan and the scent of melting cheese and roasted chicken, caramelized onions and a subtle undercurrent of salsa verde rose up from the pan. She inhaled memories.

The doorbell rang again.

"I'll get it." Caroline went through the house to the front door. "Marion's here," she called out.

"With the last tomatoes from my garden," Marion said, standing in the doorway, her hair loose and silver. "Hello, darling Kate." Marion took Kate in her arms and held her for a long moment.

Behind Marion came two younger women, one of them with a cake in her hands.

"Sara, did you bake that?" Kate asked, surprise in her voice.

"I wish—the only thing I've put in an oven since the twins were born is chicken fingers," Sara replied, pushing her hair back from her face with her free hand.

"She wouldn't have even made it out the front door if we hadn't been carpooling," Hadley commented and handed Caroline a loaf of bread.

"Last but not least," a voice came from the bottom of the stairs. "I'm no cook," Daria said as she entered, all red hair and curls, handing a bottle to Kate, "but I know a good wine when I see one. Now, can we start celebrating?"

THE PLATES WERE ALMOST EMPTY, the light gone early from the September sky. The edges of Kate's patio were lost in the foliage beyond, its contours lit by the back porch light and the candles on the wrought iron table, around which the women sat, talking with the ease of those who have settled into one another's lives. Out on the road the occasional car drove by, the sound muffled by the laurel hedge that held the garden within its green walls. Everything felt softened, the garden more smells than sights, emitting the last scents of summer into the air.

Kate looked at the women around her. It was an incongruous group—it reminded Kate of a collection of beach rocks gathered over time by an unseen hand, the choices only making sense when they were finally all together. Daria and Marion were sisters, Sara and Hadley neighbors; Kate and Caroline had met when their children were in preschool—individual lives blending and moving apart, running parallel or intersecting for longer or shorter periods of time due to proximity or a natural affinity. It had taken the birth of Sara's twins, and then Kate's illness, to weave their dissimilar connections into a whole.

Kate heard a voice coming through the house.

"*There* you are . . ." A woman, dressed in a loose-fitting jacket and slim jeans, came out onto the back porch. "I'm sorry I'm late; my flight was delayed." She ran down the steps to the patio and hugged Kate.

"Ava," Kate said, holding her.

"Did I smell my mother's enchiladas?" Ava asked, and Kate smiled.

"I saved you some." She started for the kitchen.

"No, you don't," Caroline quickly interjected. "You're the queen tonight. You shouldn't have to wait on anybody." She sent a pointed look in Ava's direction.

"I'll get more wine," Daria added, following Caroline into the house.

Kate pulled a chair up next to her and motioned for Ava to sit down.

Now they were all here, Kate thought.

DARIA CAME OUT the back door, the glossy brochure in one hand. "Hey, what's this?" she asked. "I found it tacked to the bulletin board."

"Robin wants the two of us to go rafting down the Grand Canyon," Kate said.

"But . . . ?" Caroline had come out on the porch and was watching Kate's face.

"Have you seen those rapids?" Kate replied.

The women around the table nodded in understanding, although if they were to be honest none of them had ever experienced the Grand Canyon other than to stand on its rim and look down to the river below, which looked only green and far away from that distance. But that, of course, didn't matter. The women ranged in age, but they were all old enough to know that in the currency of friendship, empathy is more valuable than accuracy.

"It's scary," Caroline agreed, coming down the steps and setting a plate in front of Ava.

"Which is *exactly* why she should do it," Daria broke in. "Kate, you're here; you're alive. You should do something crazy to celebrate."

Kate simply shook her head and sipped from her wineglass, her thoughts traveling far from them, underwater. It was dark there, cold, where the waves grabbed you and took your life where you didn't expect it to go.

"Maybe we should give her some space," Sara suggested.

The women shifted in their seats. Ava picked up her fork and took a bite of enchilada, closing her eyes in happiness. Kate smiled, watching her.

"All right," Marion said, leaning forward. "Here's a thought. Kate, when is the trip?"

"Next August." Kate regarded Marion suspiciously.

"Well, then," Marion continued calmly. "I propose we make a pact. If Kate agrees to go down the Grand Canyon, we'll each promise to do one thing in the next year that is scary or difficult or that we've always said we were going to do but haven't." She scanned the circle. "Everybody in?"

The women looked about at each other. One by one, they nodded in agreement.

Marion turned to Kate.

"All right?" she asked.

It was still for a moment. On the other side of the hedge, a car door opened with an electronic beep; the jingle of a dog's collar passed by.

"All right," Kate replied finally—and then she smiled. "But here's the deal. I didn't get to choose mine, so I get to choose yours."